KT-379-929

PUFFIN BOOKS

War Dog

Martin Booth was born in Lancashire and lived in Hong Kong from 1950 to 1964, where he began his education. He is married with two children and now lives in a seventeenth century house in Somerset. He travels very widely and returns to Hong Kong at least once a year.

WAR DOG

Martin Booth

PUFFIN BOOKS

For Julian

PUFFIN BOOKS

Published by the Penguin Group
Penguin Books Ltd, 27 Wrights Lane, London W8 5TZ, England
Penguin Putnam Inc., 375 Hudson Street, New York, New York 10014, USA
Penguin Books Australia Ltd, Ringwood, Victoria, Australia
Penguin Books Canada Ltd, 10 Alcorn Avenue, Toronto, Ontario, Canada M4V 3B2
Penguin Books (NZ) Ltd, 182–190 Wairau Road, Auckland 10, New Zealand

Penguin Books Ltd, Registered Offices: Harmondsworth, Middlesex, England

First published by Hamish Hamilton Ltd 1996
Published in Puffin Books 1998
3 5 7 9 10 8 6 4

Copyright © Martin Booth, 1996
All rights reserved

The moral right of the author has been asserted

Filmset in Bembo

Made and printed in England by Clays Ltd, St Ives plc

Except in the United States of America, this book is sold subject to the condition that it
shall not, by way of trade or otherwise, be lent, re-sold, hired out, or otherwise
circulated without the publisher's prior consent in any form of binding or cover other
than that in which it is published and without a similar condition including this
condition being imposed on the subsequent purchaser

British Library Cataloguing in Publication Data
A CIP catalogue record for this book is available from the British Library

ISBN 0–140–37860–X

*D*uring the Second World War, the armed forces were allowed to requisition whatever might be needed to assist with the war effort.

Trucks and private cars were taken over. Factories were ordered to manufacture essential military supplies. Private houses, most often country estates, were occupied as military offices, billets or training camps. Private aircraft were handed over to the RAF and private leisure boats were passed to the control of the Royal Navy.

What is not generally known is that animals were also requisitioned. Racing pigeons were used as message carriers whilst horses and mules were taken for cavalry mounts or pack animals.

Even less known is the fact that, in some instances, pet dogs were requisitioned, too.

This is the story of Jet, a black Labrador cross bitch, who served her country . . .

PART ONE

AUGUST 1939–MAY 1940

O ver Crayham Woods, the new moon was a thin white sickle, bathing the fields in flat, grey light. A low mist hovered over the grass and the distant sea shimmered below the cliffs of the Dorset coast. Every now and then, some way up the hill, an owl hooted mournfully from a copse of oaks in the middle of a meadow. There was not the merest hint of a breeze. A mile away in Crayham, the church clock chimed twice.

At the edge of the woods, a shadow moved. It was a dense shadow which progressed along the tree line, cautiously, stealthily. A short way to its right another smaller, more compact – more furtive – shadow followed it.

The larger shadow belonged to a man wearing black moleskin trousers, a chocolate brown shirt and a loose-fitting dark grey jacket: he cradled a shotgun under his arm. By a blackberry bush, he lowered a sack gently to the ground, tucking it silently under the snagging branches.

'Come, Jet.'

His voice was less than a whisper.

Entering the wood, the other shadow followed him and moved into a beam of moonlight. It was a black bitch about two years old, her eyes glinting like the steel shotgun barrels.

They moved without so much as a cracking twig or ruffled leaf towards a clearing. At the edge of the moon-shadows, they simultaneously halted, alert. All was still: then something moved beneath a tall elm. It was a pheasant feebly flapping, its head stuck in a cardboard cone.

'Never fails, Jet,' the man murmured. 'A few raisins, a pixie's hat and a pot of glue.'

He leaned his shotgun against the elm, Jet automatically guarding it. Kneeling by the bird, the man removed the blindfold, the bird ruffling its feathers indignantly. It would have chirked with annoyance but, within a second, the man had wrung its neck. From behind the elm came another rustle. The man did not hear it but the dog did. She growled, her hackles rising.

There was a loud explosion. The night was temporarily lit by flame. Sparks drifted in the air. A powerful torch illuminated the man, the dog, the shotgun and the pheasant.

'Don't you move now, Fred Parry,' a stern voice ordered. 'Not one jot. We're all around you.'

'Right, lads!' another voice called out. 'We've got him!'

Very slowly, Fred rose to his feet as a police sergeant appeared out of the night. He was accompanied by two gamekeepers. The policeman shone his torch on Jet. Fred nodded to her and she lay down. A third, large man approached, his shotgun smoking. When he broke open the barrels, a cartridge flicked out to fall into the dry leaves.

'Evening, Sergeant Cobb, Thomas Western, Bob Stark. And not forgetting Bailiff Trott,' Fred greeted them all politely, a wry smile on his lips. He and the bailiff had been playing fox-and-hens with each other for three years. The bailiff was usually the hens.

'It'll be some time before you poach Sir Arthur's woods again,' the bailiff replied. Then, turning to one of the men, he ordered, 'Thomas, put a rope on the dog.'

Jet growled softly, watching her master's face. Fred nodded again and she quietened as a length of line was run through her collar. At the same time, Sergeant Cobb slipped a pair of handcuffs on Fred's wrists.

'That's better,' the bailiff said. 'Both trussed.' He tossed his gun to one of the gamekeepers. 'Now take the dog down the quarry and shoot it.'

For a moment, no one moved: then Fred struggled, tugging to get at the bailiff.

'You can't do that!' he yelled. 'That's my Jet . . .'

'Like hell I can't!' retorted the bailiff. 'The dog's been worrying sheep.'

'She hasn't . . .' Fred snapped.

'You prove that?' Bailiff Trott asked, his voice soft with menace. 'I've seen a black dog about our sheep. So has Thomas here. Haven't you, Thomas? And Bob there. We'd swear it was this dog. Wouldn't we, boys?'

'Yes, sir,' Thomas and Bob chanted dutifully.

'And landowners are in their rights to shoot sheep worrying dogs,' the bailiff concluded. 'So that's that. Shoot the animal.'

'Sorry, Harry,' Sergeant Cobb interrupted, 'but you

can't shoot the dog. Strictly speaking, it's an exhibit. Added proof of intent to poach.' He turned to Fred. 'As for you, you have the right to remain silent, but anything you might say may be taken down and used in evidence.'

Bailiff Trott glowered, knowing he had to obey the policeman. Grunting his begrudging assent, he took his gun back and the five men and the dog set off along a woodland path, heading for Crayham Lane.

At seven o'clock, Sergeant Cobb unlocked the cell door and entered with some toast, a boiled egg and a mug of tea on a tray. Fred was lying on the bunk with a grey blanket folded under his head, staring at the barred window high above his head.

'Here's your breakfast,' the policeman declared, placing the tray on the foot of the bunk. 'Come ten-thirty, you're in front of the magistrate.'

Fred sat up. 'Who's it to be?' he asked.

Sergeant Cobb grinned and answered, 'Mr Speight.'

'Old Spite himself,' Fred thought aloud. 'I've not a hope, have I?'

'No.' The policeman shook his head. 'Not a prayer.'

'So you reckon I'll go down this time?'

'As sure as the sun shines. Mr Speight's a retired head-master. Thinks the county's his classroom. This is your third time and he plays golf with Sir Arthur. He'll give you four months in the clink if he gives you a day.'

Through the window came the rattle of a chain and the sound of water being poured into a tin receptacle. Fred picked up a teaspoon from the tray but did not use it. He looked up at the window.

'Breakfast time for your accomplice, too,' Sergeant Cobb remarked.

With the teaspoon, Fred sliced the top off the boiled egg but he did not start to eat it: the yolk ran down the shell onto the side of the egg-cup.

'Will you mind my dog while I'm inside?' Fred asked quietly. His words were almost a plea. 'See she's not destroyed . . . Find her a good home . . . Temporarily, you understand.'

'I'll do my best, see she comes to no harm.'

'Her name's Jet,' Fred said. 'She's not a criminal. She's done no wrong. She's house-trained, she likes children. Doesn't snap.'

At nine o'clock, Fred was marched outside in handcuffs to a black police van. As he mounted the step, he cast a quick glance across the police station yard. Jet was tethered by a chain, sitting on her haunches and watching him. Her ears were up, her head tilted on one side as if she was trying to work out what was going on.

'Happen I'll not be seeing her for a while,' Fred said to the constable by the van. 'Do you mind . . .?'

The constable looked at Sergeant Cobb who briefly nodded. Fred walked over to Jet, squatting down before her. He put his hands out to stroke her head, the handcuffs rattling. She sniffed the strange metal around his wrists. Fred wondered if she was trying to understand why he was caught in a snare like a rabbit.

'You be a good girl, Jet,' he murmured as he ran his

hands down the smooth crown of her skull. Then, reaching under her chest, he tickled her flesh, his fingers almost but not quite pinching her; she liked that. 'Don't cause no trouble. When I get out, I'll come back for you.'

Jet wagged her tail against the dusty tarmac of the police station yard and licked Fred's cheek. There was a familiar smell about her master which she instantly recognised: it was the scent of Young's gun oil, the sweat in his shirt and moleskin trousers, mingled with the faint perfume of pheasant and hare. He smoothed her ears back so her face looked sleek, almost like a seal's, her eyes pulled into thin lines. She liked that, too.

'Time to go, Fred,' Sergeant Cobb called. 'Better not to keep Old Spite waiting.'

Fred stood up. Jet gazed at his face, waiting for the command to follow, yet it did not come. Instead, she watched as her master walked away, his steps dragging as if he was tired after a long night's poaching in the woods. By the time he reached the police van, the order had still not come. Despite her training, despite his always having taught her not to make a sound unless instructed, she made a little whimper to remind him she was there and ready for the next command.

Fred did not look back nor did he speak to her. He just stepped slowly into the van. There were tears in his eyes, which he wiped away with his thumb as the door shut out the light.

At ten-thirty precisely, Fred stepped into the dock of the magistrates' court. Old Spite and a crab-faced woman wearing a tweed jacket and heavy brogues sat on the bench. The magistrate was short and sharp. He heard the charge, briefly scowled at Fred, muttered something to Crab-face who leered in Fred's general direction, then barked out, 'Remanded in custody.'

For a week, Jet stayed in the police station yard. Sergeant Cobb provided her with a large wooden box for a kennel. On the third day, a woman holding a small boy by the hand came to see her. She peered into Jet's mouth, lifted her tail and ran her fingers the wrong way up her fur. The boy painfully tugged on one of her ears.

'It's a handsome animal,' the woman declared, her inspection done, 'but not what you put in the advertisement. It's hardly a house dog, is it?'

'She's house-trained,' Sergeant Cobb announced defensively.

'Not what I meant,' the woman retorted, adding, 'I'm afraid it simply won't do. A poacher's dog . . . One never knows what tricks it's learnt.'

She walked out of the yard, her high heels tapping on the cobbles. Sergeant Cobb shrugged and went over to the police station notice-board, opening the glass window and re-positioning a square of white card.

On the morning of Jet's eighth day in the yard, the policeman came over and squatted next to her, stroking her smooth black head.

'Well,' he said, 'what're we going to do with you? You've had no takers, you can't live here and Mrs Cobb's got two Siamese. She – and they – wouldn't take kindly to you.'

A constable leaned out of a window and shouted, 'Sergeant! Sergeant! Mr Chamberlain's coming on the wireless now.'

Sergeant Cobb stood up, tickled Jet behind her ears, and said, 'Mustn't miss what the Prime Minister's going to say.'

Jet settled into her box. The sun beat down on the wood, which gave off a strong scent of pine resin, reminding her of the woods she and Fred had so frequently patrolled at dead of night. From the window came the sound of urgent words on a radio. Jet dozed, but not for long. No sooner had the radio been switched off than the policemen started to hurry about their tasks. One began to paste strips of sticky tape over the window-panes. Another came out and, balancing on a chair, removed the bulb from the blue lamp above the door. At four o'clock, a lorry arrived and three men started to unload small sacks of sand, which were piled up like a wall in front of the main entrance.

It was nearly seven o'clock before Sergeant Cobb unclipped Jet's chain and said, 'Right, my girl. We're going out.'

He led her out of the yard and down the street, passing first a chemist's shop, then a bakery. The baker was closing up as they reached his door.

'Evening, Jim,' the baker greeted them. 'That Parry's dog?'

'That's the one,' the policeman answered. 'I'm looking to place her. You need a guard-dog?'

Jet sniffed the pavement and the man's trousers. They

smelled of flour, raisins, suet and sugar. She recognised the raisins.

'No, thank you,' he replied. Then, locking the shop door, he slipped the key into his pocket and asked, 'You hear Mr Chamberlain's broadcast?'

'It was bad news,' Sergeant Cobb agreed. 'Just like 1914. We're back fighting the Germans. Kaiser Wilhelm then, Herr Hitler now.'

Jet looked up. The policeman was gazing across the street, but he had a distant look in his eyes.

'I did my bit, Stan,' he continued. 'In The Great War. Lost a lot of my pals. The mustard gas got me in the end . . .' He fell silent and thoughtful for a moment before perking up. 'No use moping about it now. What'll be will be.'

Waving the baker good-bye, he and Jet carried on down the road. Just before the church, the policeman tugged gently on Jet's chain.

'This way, Jet,' he said kindly. 'Time we did something with you,' and, at that, he turned into a lane heading towards the Lamb & Lion.

The snug bar was packed. Farmers and shopkeepers, the doctor and the bank manager, the primary school head-master, even the Methodist minister who regularly preached against the demon drink were all there, jostling and talking at the tops of their voices. There was only one topic of conversation – Hitler and Germany.

Sergeant Cobb elbowed his way to the bar, Jet following him closely. She was not bothered by the crowds for she had been in the pub before. In fact, she recognised one of the drinkers, Mr Clerkwell; he was the town butcher whose premises she had visited more than once with Fred, always just before dawn, to deliver hares or rabbits and maybe a pheasant or two. He had always patted her and given her a scrap of liver, a scrag-end of mutton or a piece of stringy beef: yet now, he ignored her when she nuzzled his hand.

'Usual, Sergeant Cobb?' the publican greeted the policeman.

The sergeant removed his helmet, balanced it on the bar, nodded and said, 'I'm off duty now. Pint of stout, if you please.'

'So, Jim, what do you think?' asked a man in a sports jacket with leather elbow patches. 'All over by Christmas? After all, we beat the Hun in 1918. No different now.'

Sergeant Cobb did not reply until he had sipped the froth off his glass of stout. Then he said quietly, 'A lot different. This time they've got organised. Hitler's Third Reich has got more ships and tanks, submarines, lorries and men than we have. And dive-bombers. You think what those Stukas did in the civil war in Spain – then consider what a squadron could do to Southampton or Bristol or Liverpool.'

'That's defeatist talk,' someone exclaimed loudly.

Everyone fell silent. The whole town knew Sergeant Cobb had won the Military Cross in 1917. He was the town hero and no one could accuse him of being a defeatist.

'That's a realist talking,' Sergeant Cobb responded solemnly and he put his glass down. 'But now I have your attention, I want someone here to do me a favour.' He turned to Jet who was lying down beneath a bar stool. 'Up, Jet!' he ordered. 'Sit!'

Jet sat up, her tail slightly wagging on the floor, her eyes fixed on Mr Clerkwell who was holding a sausage roll. He avoided her gaze and she realised he was not in a giving mood.

'Now,' Sergeant Cobb began, 'I've got this fine young dog here who needs a home. She's well trained, house-broken as well, has a sweet nature and is good with young-sters. She'd make a fine pet and I'm sure she could be a good guard dog. If Jerry starts sending in parachutists, I'm sure she'll do her bit like the rest of us. Would anyone give her a home?'

No one answered.

'Come along,' Sergeant Cobb cajoled, like a fairground tinker, 'who'll have this fine and handsome animal? No charge. She's free to a good and caring home. She'll play with the children . . .'

'And the ducks and the geese and the hens and the lambs,' called out a voice from the rear of the bar. 'That's Fred Parry the poacher's hound.'

At this revelation, the farmers all roared with laughter and the bank manager called out, 'She'll probably blow my vault,' which caused more hilarity.

As the laughter subsided, an elderly woman standing next to Mr Clerkwell with a glass of port and lemon said, 'If this war gets going, we'll have trouble enough feeding ourselves and our children, never mind a dog as well.'

This sobering thought quietened everyone. Sergeant Cobb raised his glass from the bar but he did not drink from it. Instead, he looked down at Jet. She glanced up at him. He was suddenly very sad.

'You'd best take her to the vet,' advised the publican. 'He'll put her down for you.'

No one spoke. The thought of having such a handsome animal destroyed struck a chord in them: more than one person considered how the poacher's dog might be just the first casualty of war the town would suffer.

'I'll have her,' a voice suddenly said.

Everyone turned. Pushing through the crowd of drinkers was an army officer, his khaki uniform neatly pressed, the brass buttons on his jacket shining in the light. On his shoulder was a brass crown. He knelt by Jet, stroking her head with his left hand as his right raised her lips to display her teeth.

'Young dog,' he remarked. 'In good condition.' His hand felt under her belly, his fingers probing her stomach muscles. 'Very good condition,' he added. Then he stood up.

'Might I ask your name, sir?' Sergeant Cobb enquired.

'Major Sassoon,' the officer replied. 'You say this was a poacher's dog? And I suppose he's currently residing in one of His Majesty's special hotels?'

'On remand, sir. Sure to be sent down for a stretch.'

'I see. And you have to dispose of the dog. Tell me, why have you not had her put to sleep?'

'I made a promise to her owner . . .' Sergeant Cobb began. 'And she's a good dog. You can't blame her for her master's sins. She's well trained,' he added, as if embarking upon his sales pitch once more.

'So I can see,' said Major Sassoon. 'I will take her.'

'Going to hunt Jerry with her?' asked the publican. A few people laughed at this quip.

'In a manner of speaking, yes,' the officer replied matter-of-factly. 'I am a requisitioning officer and we are currently requisitioning dogs. Usually pets,' he added, letting the fact sink into his listeners, several of whom exchanged worried looks. 'For the war effort. Taking this one will save someone else – one of you good folk here, perhaps – from losing their own animal.' He turned to Sergeant Cobb. 'You say her name is Jet?'

'Yes, sir.'

'Well, Jet,' said the major, bending over to briefly pat her neck, 'You're in the army from now on.'

Sergeant Cobb handed over the chain and, knowing it was what Fred would have said, told her, 'You be a good girl, Jet.' Then, turning to Major Sassoon, he asked, 'What shall I tell her owner? When he comes out of prison? Where can he collect her?'

'Tell him,' the major interrupted brusquely, 'his dog has gone to serve its country. As for collecting her,' he smiled rather bleakly, 'I'm afraid that won't be possible.'

With that, the officer glanced down at Jet and snapped, 'Heel.' She stood up and followed him out the door, everyone in the bar watching her go.

The kennel block was a low building with twenty kennels on either side of a long passageway. Each had a run enclosed in wire mesh and a sleeping quarter with a raised wooden platform, upon which was strewn a thick layer of straw. In the corner by the door to the passageway was a tin bowl of water.

On her first night, Jet slept uneasily. She was used to darkness but a light shone under the door all the time and there was a peculiar, sharp smell about the concrete floor. Dogs in neighbouring kennels barked at every noise, or howled forlornly. One intermittently yapped. Every time the sentry walked along the end of the runs the Alsatian next door growled threateningly, to which the soldier muttered, 'Shut up, you dumb mutt!'

Eventually, Jet fell asleep, only to be rudely awakened by someone shouting, 'Wakey wakey, doggies! Rise and shine!' which set some of the dogs off again, calling and baying.

Some minutes later, Jet's door was opened by a young man in khaki trousers and a vest with heavy boots on his feet. He was carrying a white enamel jug. Jet got up, stretched and hesitantly wagged her tail. The soldier squatted down, putting the jug on the floor.

'Hello, girl!' he said, holding his hand out, palm upwards: he knew every dog in the world was wary of a down-facing palm. Such a hand might hit but a palm up seldom did. 'You're the newcomer, aren't you? Well, don't you worry. First night in the army's always the worst.'

He patted her head, ran his hand under her chin and briefly tickled her neck, before topping up the water bowl. Jet sniffed at it and looked hopefully at him. Fred always fed her first thing in the morning before their day in the fields.

'Looking for scoff?' the soldier asked. 'Army rule book: Dog, War, Training of, Section 15, paragraph 73. Dogs get scoff in the late afternoon. Sorry, girl,' he patted her once more and stood up, 'King's Regulations.'

At about nine o'clock, the door opened again and another soldier appeared. He did not speak, but removed Jet's collar, replacing it with a harness to which was attached a small metal disc. Clipping a leather leash to this, he gave it a little jerk.

Jet was led down the passageway and across a wide lawn of trimmed grass surrounded by white painted stones. It seemed as if every blade of grass had had a different dog mark it with its scent. On the far side of the lawn was a building built on brick piers. They went up some wooden steps and into a large room with a heavy wooden table in the centre. An army vet in a white coat stood by a sink washing his hands.

'Which one's this, corporal?' he asked, turning to pick up a towel.

'D67, sir! Came in yesterday evening, sir!'

'Do you have the B270?'

'Sir!' the soldier replied and took a folded form from his pocket.

'Hmm!' the vet pondered. 'Our first requisitioned animal. Seems the owner's been a naughty boy. Well, lift her onto the table.'

The corporal put one arm under Jet's hind legs and the other under her chest and obeyed the order. Jet did not struggle: Fred had often picked her up like this to get her over a fence or stile wrapped in barbed wire.

'She seems a good-tempered beast, corporal. We don't want another like that Airedale yesterday.'

'No, sir! Totally unsuited for military use that one. Untrainable, sir.'

The vet approached the table and stroked Jet's back, running his hand from her head right down to her tail.

'Good girl,' he assured her. 'I'm just going to give you the once-over.'

For ten minutes, he studied her teeth, turned her ears inside out, felt around the base of her tail, squeezed her nipples and spread her eyes open, peering into her mouth and stroking her coat the wrong way to see the condition of her skin. At last he wrote some notes on the form. Then, turning to the soldier, said, 'Well, this one's certainly just what we need.'

He crossed the room to a cupboard, from which he removed a small tray containing some scissors and a wooden box. He fiddled about with this for a minute, referring to the form as he did so. At last he came towards Jet and said, 'Well, D67, this'll only hurt for a moment. Will you do the honours, corporal?'

The soldier lifted Jet off the table, made her sit, slipped a muzzle over her nose and straddled her, gripping her harness tightly. The vet carefully shaved the fur away from the inside of her left ear, dabbing some methylated spirits on the bald patch. Jet wrinkled her nose at it and sneezed into the muzzle. Next, a tiny needle was inserted into her ear; Jet flinched.

'All right, girl,' the vet comforted her, as he rubbed another strange-smelling black substance on her ear.

Producing what looked to Jet like the pliers Fred used to cut snare wire, he placed her ear between the two prongs and squeezed the handles. The pliers snapped down and a sharp quick pain ran through her ear.

'That's it,' the vet said. 'All over. Now you're tattooed. You're officially D67.'

The inspection over, Jet was led into a long, wide room at the end of which half-a-dozen soldiers were sitting on a bench.

'Well, which one of you layabouts is having this little killer?' the corporal enquired. 'D67, bitch, Lab cross. About two years old.'

One of the soldiers stood up.

'That's mine, sir,' he said.

He stepped smartly forward. The corporal handed him the leash.

'Well, Lance-Corporal Turpin, she's all yours. Introduce yourself. First training session 10.30 hours.'

At the other end of the camp was a cricket field and a pavilion. The soldier took Jet around the boundary line and sat on the bottom step of the pavilion with her sitting facing him. He was a short man with close-cropped hair and ears which were too big. He held Jet's head in his hands and looked her straight in the eye.

'You and me are together now,' he said. 'Got to be a team. Work alongside each other. The sergeant shouts an order, the corporal jumps. The corporal shouts an order and I jump. When I give a command, you obey. Got it? If you don't, we're both on defaulters.'

Jet cocked her head to one side. His words were stern but not harsh.

'So what're you going to call it, Turpy?' asked a voice.

Turpin looked up. Another soldier was walking over to them with a smooth-coated collie trotting at his side.

'Hello, Singer,' Turpin greeted him. 'I haven't decided yet. Only just picked it up from the vet.' For a moment, he looked at Jet then said, 'Well, it's obvious, isn't it? My name's Turpin, just like the highwayman . . .' He leaned forward and pressed his dry, warm nose against her cold, wet one. '. . . so you're my black Bess.'

Jet, with a dozen other dogs accompanied by their handlers, formed a line across a parade ground. In front of them stood a sergeant major, the peak of his cap short, angled and shining in the sun. Under his arm he grasped a leather document case.

'Right!' he yelled. 'First test, sort the dogs from the goats. Sergeant Perkins! Battle Inoculation, in your own time!'

'Sir!' a voice barked in reply from behind the line.

There was a pause, then four light reports rang out in quick succession. Most of the dogs turned their heads. One, an Irish terrier, jumped and spun round and yapped hysterically. Jet did nothing. She had heard gunfire before: Fred's shotgun had always been much closer and certainly much louder.

Turpin reached down and patted Jet's neck, saying, 'Good girl, Bess.'

'Private Roland! Dismiss! Take your Ulsterman away.'

Private Roland came to attention and, leading his dog which was still barking, marched off in the direction of the kennels.

'Next,' the sergeant-major continued, 'you all know the basic commands. Spread out and see what your dogs know.'

Turpin took Jet across the parade ground, leading her by a short leash. She trotted quite happily by his side. When they reached the perimeter road, he stopped with Jet in front of him.

'Sit!' he ordered.

She promptly sat, watching his face. He smiled broadly, praised her and said, 'Good girl, Bess. Now,' he went on, 'down!'

Jet went down on her belly, her front legs out in front of her. She still looked Turpin in the face.

'Well, I'll be jiggered!' exclaimed Turpin, adding, 'Heel!'

Jet got up, walked round Turpin and sat down next to him, on his left with her shoulder next to his knee. She no longer gazed up at him, but looked across the parade ground where the other handlers were tugging on leashes, pressing their dogs' rumps down to make them sit or pulling their front legs from under them to make them lie.

At the command, *Stay*, Turpin let Jet's leash drop from his fingers as he walked off twenty paces, not looking back. She remained until he turned, looked at her and said, quietly, 'Come!' Jet rose and trotted smartly towards him, taking up the heel position.

'Magical!' Turpin could hardly contain himself. 'I've got a dog that knows the ropes! All the other poor muckers'll have weeks of basic training.' He knelt at Jet's side and said, 'You and me are going to get along famously. Let's show what you can do.'

The sergeant-major watched Jet go through her paces and was as impressed as Turpin.

'You've a fine animal there, Turpin,' he declared. 'She'll do you credit. What do you think of her character?'

'I've only collected her this morning, but she seems pretty intelligent and she seems to have a nice temperament. Took no notice at all of the BI shots.'

'What's her number?'

'D67, sir.'

The sergeant flicked through the papers in his document case then remarked, 'Here's your reason. The dog's last owner was a poacher. That bitch'll be better trained than any of them here.' He replaced the papers and pondered for a moment before going on. 'You know, we've been told to turn out two infantry patrol dogs. With her background, I'll bet she's just right for it.'

The next day, Jet embarked upon a course of specialist training, starting at 07:30 hours when Turpin arrived at her kennel.

'Hello, Bess D67,' he greeted her. 'Today's the day we really make a go of it.' He gave her a stroke, patted her ribs, then brushed her coat and checked her paws before slipping her a dry biscuit. Jet wagged her tail and, swallowing the biscuit, had a quick drink from her water bowl. 'Strictly against King's Regs,' Turpin whispered. 'Don't let on or we won't half cop it.'

At 09:15 hours, they mustered on parade. Only two other dogs were present. One was a grey Alsatian bitch called Tina, the other a mongrel named Scrappy. With Jet, they were the only dogs sufficiently advanced in basic training to move on to the next stage and had already been assigned their specialist tasks. Tina was to be a VP, or Vulnerable Point, dog which was what the army termed a guard dog. With her handler, a private, she was quiet and obedient but when anyone else approached, she gave a low, warning grumble, her lips lifting just a fraction to show her canine teeth. Scrappy the mongrel had an altogether different role to fulfil: he was to spend his training working his way over ploughed fields and footpaths, nosing at sods of earth, snorting at stones, snuffling at potholes and sniffing at tufts of stubble. His battlefield role was to be to detect buried mines, his eager nostrils tuning themselves over the weeks to the tang of metal and the acrid aroma of explosives.

The extra commands Jet was given to learn – *Seek* and *Leave* – were already well known to her. Fred had used them often enough when a pheasant he had shot fell into cover or a hare had bolted into a thicket. However, there was one difference: Fred had expected her to find something and then bring it back. When he said *Leave*, she just dropped whatever she was holding in her mouth at his feet. With Turpin, this was definitely not the idea.

On her first test, Jet was sent to locate a man hiding in a field of long grass. She and Turpin advanced through the grass with Jet ranging ahead of him on a long pilot rope.

At first she had no idea what she was looking for: all Turpin had said was, 'Seek.'

As they reached the middle of the field, however, she caught the strong scent of a man upon the light breeze tickling the grass-heads. She stopped and faced upwind. As a patrol dog, she should then have remained pointing towards the source of the smell, but with Fred's training behind her, once she had the direction identified, she set off after it, intent on retrieving it for her master.

'Leave! Sit!' Turpin commanded in a loud voice. Jet, unused to being halted in mid-track, carried on. 'Leave! Sit!' he ordered again, more loudly. 'Bess! Sit!'

A little confused at this – after all, she reasoned, the man might get away just like a hare might, streaking off through the grass never to be found again – Jet sat. Turpin came up alongside her, coiling in the rope.

'Good girl, Bess,' he praised her. 'But you don't go charging off! If that was an enemy patrol you and me would be done for.' He instructed her to heel, then called out, 'Right, Todger! We got you by the clump of thistles.'

About ten metres away, the grass weaved to and fro and a private stood up, frantically brushing his uniform.

'I'm covered in ants,' he wailed. 'Little red blighters. They've been stinging me for ten minutes.' He stripped off his battledress shirt and started to slap his chest, much to Turpin's amusement and Jet's curiosity.

For the rest of the afternoon, Todger, Turpin and Jet went through the same exercise, over and over. By the time she returned to the kennels, she understood exactly what was expected of her. She had to locate the direction of the target, which was always a man and never, as Turpin expressed to her several times, a rabbit or partridge of which the long grass hid a fair number. Once she had the position of the target worked out, she had to sit down, cast a glance over her shoulder at Turpin, then look in its direction. In this way, he could interpret the whereabouts of the make-believe threat Todger posed.

This was not all she learnt: she also knew now that she was called Bess. Yet still, in her mind, her real name, Jet, remained. It was not erased, merely put to the back of her consciousness, set aside for some future use, perhaps.

Gradually, as the days passed, Todger positioned himself farther and farther away until he was well over a hundred metres from the track along which Turpin led Jet. What was more, he no longer used the pilot rope, allowing her to work loose. She never failed to identify Todger's where-abouts, even when there was little breeze or when, for two days, it rained miserably from dawn to dusk.

When she was not seeking Todger she stayed at heel but, with Turpin's training, she positioned herself a little ahead of him, her head kept high so she was not confused by ground scents.

One day at the end of the third training week, Turpin did not take Jet to the grassy field. Instead, she was taken in a lorry to a wood about eight miles from the barracks. The trees were thick, with dense undergrowth between the trunks. No sooner had the lorry departed, and the stink of diesel fumes and hot gearbox oil disappeared, than Jet started to pick up the multifarious perfumes of the woodland – damp leaves, foxes, fungi, rabbits, roe deer and, by a hawthorn bush, badgers.

Every scent reminded her of her former life. By a rotting log, the faint taint of weasel brought back a night when Fred had dropped a boiled egg he was going to eat in the early hours only to have one of the little creatures zip out from under a bush, grab it and disappear. It had happened so fast even Jet did not react. The sound of a pheasant alarming way off in the woods revived thoughts of long, dark, happy nights. Yet she did not prick her ears or pay any attention to the bird. She knew she had other quarry to hunt now.

Jet and Turpin were not alone, but accompanied by a platoon of twenty soldiers under the command of a captain and a sergeant.

'Right, lads!' the sergeant said, 'This is today's exercise. We deploy through this wood. Two miles, close cover on all sides. Keep sharp! Turpin's going ahead with the dog.'

The soldiers formed two parallel ranks and set off along a narrow track. Ahead, Jet worked loose, ranging from side to side, her head up, her nose testing the air and the confusing mixture of smells. She had to ignore them all, even the warm stink of a rabbit warren close to the side of the track. Her quarry, she knew, had two legs and smelled of damp uniform, sweat, canvas webbing straps, leather and gunmetal.

They had gone about a mile when Jet paused, tested the air, obediently sat, glanced at Turpin, then stared at an oak tree some way off through the cover. Turpin raised his hand. The platoon halted as the captain made his way towards him.

'Located them?' the officer whispered.

'Dog says the enemy appear to be by the oak tree, sir. Two o'clock from the broken beech, thirty yards.'

The captain nodded and signalled the others. The platoon knelt, cocking their rifles.

Suddenly, the wood was filled with gunfire. Flashes showed in the bushes near the oak. A bright light followed by a *whoomph!* illuminated the trees. The platoon returned fire.

As soon as the shooting started, Turpin crouched by Jet's side and, instructing her to lie down, put his hand on her neck to calm her. His fingers were shivering ever so slightly and so was her neck, but it was not from fear. Both man and dog were filled with the thrill of their first taste of war.

After a few minutes, the shooting ceased. The platoon reformed and continued to the end of the wood, where the soldiers who had been playing the part of the enemy were lying about in a field of wheat stubble, smoking cigarettes, chatting and drinking from their canteens.

'Here come the trigger-happy boys!' shouted a voice, as the platoon emerged from the trees.

'We got you fair and square!' shouted one of the platoon. 'We had you sussed out and no mistake.'

Turpin and Jet sat on the ground with the others and a mug of tea was handed over. Turpin poured some water from his canteen into a bowl he tugged from his pack.

'I'll have my cuppa,' he said to Jet, 'and you can have yours.'

As Jet lapped the warm water, a soldier came over and

squatted down next to her. He had blue eyes, big ears and smelled faintly of peppermint. His steel helmet was tipped back on his head showing a shock of fair hair.

'Hello, Turpy!' he said. 'This your wonder-dog they're all talking about?'

'That's my Bess, Smithy,' Turpin answered with obvious pride.

'She sure got our number. We were silent as hell and downwind as best we could be. And the sergeant issued us all with peppermint humbugs . . . Want one?' He handed a sweet to Turpin who unwrapped it and popped it in his mouth. 'Anyway, I've never seen a pooch that sharp.' He reached over to Jet. 'Well done, doggy. If we wind up across the Channel fighting Jerry, I hope you're with my lot.'

That evening, as Turpin mixed Jet's meat and biscuit in her food bowl, the sergeant-major came up and enquired, 'So how was she?'

'Brilliant, sir, just brilliant! Didn't flinch at the fighting. Sat down. She was dead accurate with her location.' He pursed his finger and thumb together, bits of biscuit sticking to the skin. 'Spot on, sir!'

'No barking, whining?'

'None, sir. Not a peep.'

They walked to the kennel, passing other handlers feeding and grooming their dogs. The sergeant-major paused to have a word with several of the men, then rejoined Turpin in Jet's kennel, sitting down on the edge of her plank bed and stretching his legs out before him. Jet looked at him, then carried on eating: after the day's exercise, she was hungry.

26

'I never thought I'd be this lucky, sir,' Turpin commented. 'You dream of getting a dog like this. One you can work with, have real confidence in.' He stroked Jet's back as she ate. 'She's reached A1 in four and a half weeks. It usually takes at least twelve . . .'

'And then there's a failure rate, too,' the sergeant-major added. 'They don't all pass muster.'

'You know, sir, I'd trust my life to this dog. To my Bess.'

The sergeant opened the flap of his breast pocket and handed a folded envelope to Turpin.

'What's this, sir?'

'Now's your chance,' the sergeant-major said. 'To trust your Bess. You're both posted to an infantry division, along with some of the other lads. You go next week.'

Turpin could hardly contain his excitement. Jet, sensing it, stopped eating and looked up.

'Where, sir? Aldershot, sir? Catterick?'

'No, lad,' the sergeant-major said quietly. 'Calais. France. With the BEF. British Expeditionary Force. You're off to face the Hun.'

For over an hour, the *Hayling Bay* rocked and bucked as waves battered her hull. Sea spray showered over the bow, drenching the men and the lorries stowed on deck. Turpin and Jet huddled under a groundsheet against a bulkhead, Smithy next to them. Just above their heads, a sailor in a sou'wester pointed his anti-aircraft gun at the miserable grey sky, on the look-out for Luftwaffe dive-bombers.

As evening was falling, they arrived at a dock, the stones

of the quayside glistening with rain. Herring gulls lined the roofs of the warehouses and perched on bollards, only taking to the wing if someone approached within three metres of them. Although it was dusk, no lights were switched on as a precaution against air raids.

Once disembarked, the soldiers marched behind the lorries through a dismal seaside town, all the houses shuttered up and seemingly abandoned to the weather and the war. Outside the built-up area, they crossed some sand dunes to a pine wood, where there was a tented transit camp hidden under trees and camouflage netting. Here, the soldiers halted and were shown into a mess tent, where they were seated for a meal of stewed beef and suet pudding, washed down with a mug of milky tea. Hardly anyone spoke. They were all too tired and just ate their food. Even Jet's appetite was blunted and she did not consume the whole of her bowl when Turpin placed it before her. When the meal was over, the soldiers were allocated their quarters. Turpin and Smithy were assigned a two-man tent. Jet curled up between them on the ground.

Turpin extinguished the tiny flame in the lantern hanging from the ridge pole. 'Not exactly the Ritz, is it?' Smithy moaned, as they hunched themselves into their sleeping bags. 'For a start, you don't share your kip with a dog in the better hotels.'

'I don't mind Bess,' Turpin responded. 'Much better her than . . .' He considered the options for a minute. '. . . Private Carter. He smells worse.'

'Accounts for his nickname,' Smithy grinned. 'Carter the Far . . .'

'Get your heads down!' a stern voice outside the tent commanded. 'This isn't a Boy Scout camp.'

The two men lay back in the darkness. From outside came the sound of stealthy footsteps as the sentries patrolled the transit camp, and the distant hoot of an owl.

'According to the billeting corporal,' Smithy said, keeping his voice low, 'there's a Froggie village about a mile away. Tomorrow, after we're stood down, I'm going to have a shiftie. Get me some pretty little French *madam-o-sell*.' He paused at the thought of the prospect, then continued, 'You coming, Turpy? Bring Bess along. Maybe she can find herself a handsome French poodle.'

Over the quiet sounds of the camp, there came a far-off, high-pitched whine. Jet opened her eyes and perked her ears. It was a sound such as she had never heard before, a cross between a whistle and a screech. Within seconds, it was followed by a distant explosion, then several others.

'Don't think we'll be going gallivanting about in any village,' Turpin remarked soberly, adding, 'if there's any village left.'

'What do you think it's going to be like?' Smithy pondered. 'The war, I mean.'

'I don't know,' Turpin said. 'Dangerous. Exciting, for sure. Damned hard work. Not too many *madam-o-sells*.'

'Have you thought . . .' Smithy began hesitantly, '. . . thought about killing someone? I mean – well, it's our job, isn't it?'

'My job – and Bess's – is to find them,' Turpin answered.

'Yes, but we've to kill them, too. That's what our Lee

Enfield's for, isn't it?' He felt by his side where his rifle was leaning against his pack. 'The bayonet's not for shaving and opening tins of bully beef. It's for opening Jerry bellies.'

'Have *you* thought about it?' Turpin rejoined.

'I have, yes,' Smithy retorted, his voice filled with menace and bravado. 'I can't wait to get a Jerry in my sights. Squeeze the trigger, take up the slack, pop one in him.'

As Bess slept and Smithy intermittently snored, Turpin lay awake, thinking over his words. He had not considered that he was meant to kill people. Of course, he had gone through basic training, been taught how to shoot a man-shaped target and thrust his bayonet into a sack of straw hanging from a wooden frame, but he had never really contemplated actually doing it. For real.

Next morning, Turpin woke at six o'clock. He quickly shaved in a basin of cold water then, after giving Jet a brief grooming, took her for an exercise walk. The sentries told him he could go anywhere in the wood, but not to venture outside it. The open fields were strictly out of bounds as the coast was frequently observed by German reconnaissance aircraft.

With Jet on her leash, they walked through the trees, passing rows of tents, parked lorries and field howitzers, piles of ammunition boxes and petrol storage drums. In one area, a row of light tanks was being attended to by mechanics, whilst in another soldiers were stripping and cleaning three-inch mortars and Vickers machine guns. There was a tension in the air, no one speaking, each man working silently on his allotted task.

When they reached the end of the woodland, fields stretched before them, lines of trim stubble over dark earth. Just in front of Jet lay a little pile of rabbit pellets which reeked: the rabbits had been using their latrine during the night. Across the other side of the field was a row of tall poplar trees, a farm-house and haystack which had toppled over.

'Just like England,' Turpin remarked, as much to Jet as to himself. 'If it weren't for that row of trees, this could be Suffolk. From the look of that hayrick, the farmer's moved out.'

As they gazed at the view from the edge of the trees, Jet discerned a humming sound: it grew louder in her ears although it was ten seconds before Turpin picked it up. When he did, he tightened his fingers on her leash.

'Come, Bess!' he ordered and he tugged her back into the trees.

The noise swelled louder and louder until it seemed to surround them: then, bursting over the poplars, a fighter appeared. It was painted grey and flying very low, close to the ground. Half-way across the field it banked, showing the zig-zag of a swastika upon one of its two tail fins. As soon as it passed over the trees, the roar of its twin engines suddenly died out.

'Messerschmitt,' Turpin said aloud, speaking almost in awe. 'He's on a recce. Taking photos.' He put his hand on Jet's head. She nuzzled her skull into his palm. 'That's the Hun, Bess,' he went on. 'That's the enemy we've come to find.'

★

At dusk that day, Turpin lifted Jet into a lorry lined up in a convoy of vehicles which stretched through the trees. Smithy and some other soldiers were already in the vehicle and Jet squeezed in between him and Turpin. At 20:00 hours, the engines started up, the lorries jerking into motion, leaving the wood to turn on to a road lined with poplar trees and ditches. None of the vehicles showed a light; each driver followed the one in front by watching a white disc painted on the rear axle. Motorcyclists rode by, yet even they had no lights on.

'How long's this going to take?' Smithy mused, after they had been driving for about an hour. 'I tried to ask the sergeant but he didn't – or wouldn't – tell me.'

'We'll arrive just before dawn,' replied a soldier sitting by the tailgate of the lorry, a tommy-gun across his lap. 'But don't ask me where!'

As first light was breaking, the lorries halted in a small village. Jet jumped down and stood sniffing the air. She could make out the soldiers she had travelled with, and the exhausts and hot engines of the lorries, but nothing else: no scent of dogs or farmyard animals, of food cooking or fires being lit. The village was deserted.

'Fall in!' ordered a sergeant. When the troops were lined up, he went on, 'We're going from here north-east for about three miles. No talking, no smoking. Not even belching. We're that close to Jerry's front line, he can tell the colour of your underwear.'

The soldiers set off, marching in silence, only the noise of their boots on the soil giving them away. As the day-light grew stronger, a mist rose from the ground, giving them welcome cover and dulling any sound. Eventually, they reached a network of trenches dug into the side of a gentle hill. At the top of the hill was a wood of oak trees. At the bottom ran a small river across which was a large village.

'Welcome to the war, lads!' a private cheerily greeted Turpin, Smithy and Jet as they entered the trenches, which were more than three metres deep and two wide. 'This here's St Pierre-sur-Something. We call it Saint Pee. And this . . .' he smacked the side of the trench with his fist '. . . is the main rear trench. We call it Oxford Street. Main road. Get it?' He grinned. 'Supplies kept here, ammo, medical stuff, scoff. And we live here. You lot are billeted just down there, first trench on the left. Dog and handler's kennel is second hole along in the ground.'

Turpin led Jet along the trench and found their dugout. It was a square cave cut into the side of the trench about two and a half metres wide and three deep, but only a metre and a half high. Over the entrance hung a curtain of stiff, filthy canvas. The previous occupant had left an oil lamp in a blackened niche on the wall and half a bale of hay.

'Well, this is our new home, Bess,' Turpin exclaimed as he spread the hay around for both of them to lie on. 'Not much, is it?'

Jet wagged her tail, sniffed the hay, lay down and started to lick her paws. The trench was five centimetres deep with mud and it had collected between her pads. After an hour, the cheery private came round with mugs of tea, thick chunks of bread and cheese, and a bone to which clung some scraps of meat.

'Cha and wedges!' he exclaimed in a jolly voice. 'And a bit of dead horse for Private Dog.'

The bone kept Jet busy until the soldiers were mustered in the main trench just before noon, to be addressed by an officer in a mud-smeared uniform.

'Right, chaps,' he began, standing on an ammunition box, but taking care his head was still well below the parapet of the trench, 'my name's Captain Blair and you're on the border between France and Belgium. We're in the section between the Maginot Line and the North Sea coast. If Jerry's going to break through, he'll have a go here. To the east of us are the forests of the Ardennes where he's massing his forces. A lot of planes fly over to recce our positions. Patrols going out over the border have encountered the enemy but we've given as good as we've got. Our current role is to maintain the line and harass Jerry with night patrols. Any questions?'

'How far away are they, sir?' asked one soldier.

'Not far. They're in possession of the village you can see across the river. They're not dug in there but about two miles back from it. The area between's a sort of no-man's-land. Any more questions?'

'Where's the nearest pub, sir?' piped up another voice.

The soldiers laughed and the officer grinned before replying, 'The Green Dragon, soldier. Next door to the cinema, just past the chippy, opposite the phone box. You can't miss it.' He became serious again. 'You'll be deployed into platoons this afternoon. We need a plan of the dead ground behind the trees east of the village. First

34

patrols go out tonight, 23:00 hours. Good luck to you and may God be with you.'

Turpin spent the rest of the day checking his equipment and grooming Jet.

'You'll have to look your best when we march into Berlin,' he told her. 'Show all those dachshunds and rottweilers what an English dog is, eh? Wouldn't do to be badly turned out.'

At 17:00 hours, he gave Jet her daily meal of meat and crushed biscuit, with a bowl of fresh water poured from her canteen. Although it was against regulations, Turpin had managed to filch a spare aluminium canteen so that they each had their own water supply. When she had eaten, he took her down the trench and into the oak wood so she could, as he put it, see to her ablutions. This done, he sat on his haunches at the entrance to their dugout to strip and meticulously clean his rifle. In a dugout opposite, Smithy was doing the same thing.

'You thinking what I'm thinking?' Smithy enquired after a while.

'I expect so,' Turpin answered. 'My life – and Bess's – is going to depend on this pop-gun. I don't want it jamming on me.'

The ten members of B Platoon huddled at the eastern end of Oxford Street. The night was pitch black with clouds scudding across the sky, briefly showing areas of brilliant starlight. A frost was forming on the ground even before the men gathered together.

'Lucky there's no moon,' Smithy murmured.

'Jerry may not see us but he'll hear us,' Turpin replied. 'Sounds carry a long way in cold air.'

At 23:00 hours, the platoon slipped over the rim of the trench and set off, crouching low, towards the river. Jet's breath steamed on the air in front of her face. She was eager, but did not strain on her leash: it was not just her training which prevented her from tugging, but also her innate sense of behaviour. She was, for the first time since that night in Crayham Woods, hunting. Really hunting. Not pheasants in blind traps – but men.

Reaching the river bank, the platoon halted in the cover of a thick reed bed. At the disturbing approach of men, several ducks ruffled their feathers. Had she been with Fred, Jet would have considered going after one, yet now she ignored them. They were nothing to her. Her quarry tonight, she knew, was bigger and more important.

Captain Blair made a hand signal. Turpin whispered to Jet and, slipping her leash, the two of them moved into the water. It was freezing and fast flowing mid-stream, but only came up to Jet's belly. Once they reached the other side, Jet shook the water off her coat and ranged along the river bank. She found nothing and returned to Turpin, who snapped his fingers. Very quietly, one by one, the soldiers waded across after them.

The next obstacle was an open field of long grass lying flat in the frost. They moved across this at a crouch, the ice tingling Jet's pads, until they came to a wood. Here, the men huddled together as Captain Blair issued his orders in a barely audible whisper.

'Clarke, take Fry and Knightley to the right. Barker, your pair left. You two,' he pointed at Smithy and a young private called Tackman, 'with me. Turpin – up front. Take point.'

Turpin quickly tousled Jet's ears and they entered the wood. The undergrowth was sparse, the ground covered with dead leaves. The frost had not yet reached under the trees so the leaves were damp and soft underfoot.

Jet's every nerve was taut. She could see well ahead in the darkness, the tree trunks standing like black pillars against the night. Twice she heard a scuttling sound but ignored it. Rats. Mice. They did not count. Keeping her head high, she continually tested the air. It was not until they reached the far end of the trees that she caught a whiff of man. She immediately sat, glanced at Turpin and stared at a bush twenty metres away. Turpin stopped, raised his arm very slowly and made a signal. Corporal Barker and his men moved forward ever so slowly, to disappear round the bush. There was a soft hush of noise, like several men sighing loudly together; then they re-appeared. Jet picked up a warm scent on the air. It was the iron-smelling odour of fresh blood.

The platoon regrouped and veered off to the left, with Jet working once more. Yet she picked up no more people. At 04:00 hours, they reached the safety of the British trench where mugs of piping hot tea were handed round. Jet gratefully lapped at her bowl, the icy cold water quickly slaking her thirst. Captain Blair joined his men.

'Well done, chaps!' he praised them. 'We've mapped the area east of the village and Barker's got his trophy.'

37

Barker held up a pistol in a leather holster and said, 'Luger, sir. One of the Jerries was an officer.'

The Captain came over to Turpin sitting at the entrance to the dug-out. Jet lay next to him on her straw. Turpin started to stand but Captain Blair said, 'Don't get up, Turpin. You're probably the most tired of us all. It's not easy being a dog handler, always making the front running. You've done very well indeed.'

'Thank you, sir,' Turpin responded.

'And so did your dog here,' the officer continued. 'It really is a remarkable animal. So quiet and well-trained. Had I not known he was with us . . .'

'She, sir,' Turpin interrupted. 'Her name's Bess.'

'Well, Bess,' Captain Blair said, lowering himself to his haunches and looking her in the eye, 'you're a damned fine dog and a credit to the regiment.'

Through the bitter, deep snow of the winter and the balmy days of early spring, Turpin and Jet patrolled the Western Front, moving with their unit to different sections of the front line. The days passed in a blur for her. From time to time, they came under enemy fire but no one was injured or killed: indeed, they were the only platoon in the regiment not to take a casualty. Everyone said this was because of Jet and her superb senses. By the end of February, the platoon was referred to by many as *Bess's Boys*.

Twice Turpin went on leave, taking Jet with him. They did not return to England, merely withdrawing fifty miles behind the lines to live in a French village. The French innkeeper with whom they were lodged insisted Jet sleep in a stable: Turpin refused point-blank. She slept in the room with him. The billeting officer defended his stand and the Frenchman had to give in.

These days of rest were wonderful for Jet. The inn was warm and smelt of fresh bread, sausages and cats. Mice scuttled in the walls at night. The chickens scattered before her in the yard. Turpin took her for long walks in the snow and, on Christmas Day, he presented her (*strictly against King's Regulations*) with a bar of dark Belgian chocolate which they shared between them.

Back at the front, it was work as usual. The months quickly passed by. Bess's Boys went into no-man's-land at least once every two days. They mapped behind enemy lines, planted mines along pathways used by German patrols, cut German field telephone wires and sabotaged German vehicles and fuel dumps.

Yet the tide of war was shifting. For them, it changed decisively one starry night in the middle of May.

Just after dark, the platoon crept forward from their lines and entered an extensive area of woodland. They followed an indistinct track made, Jet could tell from scent markings and dung, by deer. They encountered not a sign of the enemy until they came upon a clearing about one hundred and fifty metres across, in which stood a woodsman's hut. Beside it was a wide pool surrounded by sedges. Jet paused and listened, testing with her nose. She could not smell men, yet there was a strange, if slight, taint to the air she could not identify.

'What is it, Bess?' Turpin murmured in her ear, kneeling beside her in the darkness at the edge of the clearing.

She gave him a quick glance and sniffed the air again. The gentle tang was still there, untraceable. It seemed to hang in the atmosphere.

'Trouble, Turpin?' Captain Blair whispered.

'Not sure, sir,' he muttered back. 'Bess's picked up something but it's not a man.'

'She's not spooked by a fox . . .' the officer replied yet, no sooner had he spoken, he knew this was out of the question: Jet was never spooked.

No one moved. For twenty minutes, the platoon studied the clearing. Jet kept her senses honed. Then there was a movement. Everyone stared at it. A deer appeared and, stepping daintily towards the pool, dipped its head to drink.

Captain Blair smiled in the starlight. If the deer was so confident there could hardly be a squad of Jerry troops nearby. He signalled for everyone to spread out and move forward with caution.

Very slowly, the platoon set off. The deer saw them and trotted away into the shadows. Jet could hear it moving through the trees, could smell its breath lingering in the air. They reached the hut safely. Captain Blair entered it: it was empty. Meanwhile, Fry had gone round to the rear of the hut. Beside a woodpile, his boot caught on a thin wire. He tugged it. There was a loud hissing noise. Jet was startled. Suddenly, there was a pop like a cork coming out of a bottle and the clearing was floodlit by a magnesium flare. Every member of the platoon was lit up like an actor on a stage.

'Down! Down!' yelled Captain Blair.

Sparks of gunfire flickered in the far trees. Turpin fell across Jet, pressing her to the ground. Clarke returned fire with his Thomson sub-machine gun. Captain Blair lay close to Jet, firing his revolver, aiming at the far flashes. Bullets zipped through the air, splintering the walls of the hut, threshing the lower branches of the trees and bringing down showers of young leaves and unripe nuts.

After a few minutes, the flare faded, then went out, and the firing ceased. Captain Blair signalled for the platoon to pull back and they started to crawl across the grass of the clearing to the safety of the trees. Jet followed suit, creeping almost cat-like on her belly alongside Turpin. Yet Smithy did not move. He lay quite still in the grass, his head resting on his arm. He might have been taking a nap.

Turpin wriggled over to him. He was dead, a wide gash in the side of his neck, his blood already congealing on the khaki collar of his battledress. Jet snuffled at his hand. His fingers twitched as if to tickle her chin, yet they did not reach up. Turpin took hold of Smithy's rifle and they backed away.

No one criticised Jet. The Germans had been at least one hundred metres away and there was no breeze. Besides, she had sensed something. If anyone was to blame it was Captain Blair for assuming the deer was a safe sign, yet even he was excused the error. It was war and these things happened.

When they reached their own lines everyone was busy. Field telephone wires were being wound up, stores packed into boxes, ammunition stowed in lorries, the dug-outs destroyed and the trenches mined.

'We're pulling back,' a colonel informed the men, the scarlet flash on his collar like the blood on Smithy's tunic. 'Jerry's broken through five miles to the east. There's a Panzer division behind. Tanks, field artillery. We're falling back. Move out in one hour.'

The platoon was exhausted but they had to collect their belongings and see their section of trench was uninhabitable. When the tasks were done, they clambered into a lorry and set off bumping over rough fields and rutted tracks.

Jet dozed on the journey, her body swaying to the rocking motion of the vehicle, her head resting on Turpin's muddy boot. Off and on she dreamed, her paws twitching much as Smithy's fingers had.

At midday, they arrived at a camp outside a town which had been bombed. The men were assigned to tents, Turpin sharing his with Barker. The earth was wet and there were no groundsheets available, so Turpin constructed a make-shift bed for Jet out of the door from a burned-out cottage. He balanced it between two ammunition boxes and covered it with a length of sacking. It was not ideal but it did not matter: after three days, they were off again in a convoy of trucks heading westwards, through villages and hamlets where silent knots of sullen men and weeping women watched them pass. Only small children waved to them and even they did so in a lack-lustre fashion.

At three o'clock on the afternoon of the fourth day, the trucks suddenly screeched to a halt. They were on a straight road lined by trees, beyond which were deep ditches and fields which had been left fallow.

'Out! Out!' the driver shouted, swinging down from the cab and grabbing his rifle. 'Into the ditches!'

For a moment no one moved. Then came the drone of aircraft, increasing sharply in volume. Turpin glanced up. High in the blue, early-summer sky were three black dots.

'*Stukas!*' someone yelled.

There was a scramble to get out of the truck. Turpin almost threw Jet over the tailgate, landing on the ground next to her, grabbing her by her harness and yanking her into the ditch. Together, they slithered down to the muddy, ankle-deep water.

The dive bombers whistled as they hurtled downwards. The men held their helmets over their heads and pressed themselves into the sides of the ditch. Jet looked up. The first aircraft seemed to be coming straight at her, the whine in her ears growing more acute with every second until it seemed to fill her head. Her hackles instinctively rose. Her lips retracted from her teeth in a snarl. Just when she was ready to bite the aircraft should it come close enough, it swung round. Two small, black objects detached themselves from the bomber's belly. Jet cowered now. Thinking they might be stones, she got down on her haunches next to Turpin.

As the aircraft noise decreased rapidly, there were a series of loud explosions. Clouds of dirt blew over the ditch into the fields, whilst stones pattered into the water. Two of the trucks burst into flames, the doors ripping off and clattering on the road. Another vehicle, Captain Blair's Humber staff car, was blown on to its side. Further down the ditch, someone screamed.

The men waited. The aircraft noise gradually mounted again. They were not whining and diving now but flying level along the line of the road. Suddenly, shells started hitting the vehicles at the end of the convoy. They rocked from side to side under the impact. Glass shattered. Stones on the road chipped and spat. Another truck caught fire with a dull *whoosh!* as the fuel tank ignited. A motorcycle leapt high into the air and jammed in the branches of a tree.

All was quiet once more. The soldiers began, one by one, to leave the ditch and survey the damage. Not one vehicle was unscathed. The truck Turpin, Jet and the others had been riding in was riddled with jagged holes. Oil dripped on to the road and three of its tyres were flat.

'Well, that's scotched the transport,' Private Fry said morosely. 'We're down to Shank's pony from here on.'

Collecting what personal equipment was not damaged, the troops lined up and set off in a ragged line. Jet kept to heel. The sun shone down on them, warming Jet's fur and making her feel contented, yet it did little to raise the men's spirits. They were, they now knew, members of a defeated army.

Late in the afternoon, as they marched along the road, Clarke said, as much to himself as to Turpin and the others, 'You know where we're heading, don't you, muckers? We're heading back to Blighty. To good old England.'

'Don't be daft, Nobby,' Tackman retorted. 'We aren't due any leave for weeks.'

'Maybe,' Clarke replied, 'but you take a quick squint up there.'

The platoon looked up. Flying across the sky were V formations of birds.

'Seagulls,' Clarke announced. 'That means we're near the coast.'

In a quarter of an hour, they passed through a roadblock manned by sentries and covered by a Bren gun post, crested a low hill and beheld a sight which both astonished and terrified them.

Along a wide beach, as far as the eye could see in either direction, were thousands upon thousands of soldiers. They had no tents, no vehicles for shelter. They just sat on the sand, squatted around small fires, or lay in shallow trenches. At the top of the beach, where there were some trees, thousands more were milling around or sitting in groups.

A soldier came past them, carrying a bucket of water.

'Hey, mate!' Clarke asked. 'Where . . .? What the hell's going on?'

Yet the soldier just stared at them and walked on, the water spilling.

Tackman had his map out and orientated it to the panorama before them, glancing up to check the landmarks.

'I know,' he said quietly. 'See over there. That town? That's here.' He jabbed his finger on the map.

The others leaned over. Printed on the map was one word – *Dunkirk*.

Within an hour of arriving, Turpin had dug himself and Jet a slit trench in which to take shelter. It was about half a metre deep and L-shaped, with Jet in one leg and Turpin in the other, their heads meeting at the angle.

'It's not going to be any good in a direct hit,' Turpin said to her as he dug into the sand with an entrenching spade, 'but it'll serve us well the rest of the time.'

For two days, they occupied the trench, as thousands more soldiers arrived in trucks, on foot, in staff cars – even on bicycles 'borrowed' from villages along the way. Every one of them was weary to the point of exhaustion. Many were wounded. The worst were accommodated in tents pitched under the trees: the remainder lay on the sand, tended by their comrades. At night, the gentle wind blowing off the sea carried the groans and grunts of injured men.

Close to the slit trench, one man lay with a bad wound in his thigh. Turpin changed his dressing every few hours and held the man's head up so he could drink but, as the hours past, his wound began increasingly to stink.

'He's a goner,' Turpin whispered to Jet in the darkness of their second night on the beach. He was keen to talk to her for there was no one else in whom he could confide. The other members of the platoon had moved off and become lost in the crowds. 'He's got gas gangrene in his leg. No one survives that.'

Sure enough, in the morning, the man was dead and Turpin, ordering Jet to stay, left her to find a padre. It was whilst he was gone that the first strafing flight came over. For an hour, wave upon wave of German aircraft flew above the beach, dropping bombs and firing their cannons into the throngs of soldiers, few of whom could fire back for they had little if any ammunition left.

During the strafing, Jet curled up in her trench. Pieces

of hot shrapnel seared the air, splattering into the sand around her. When a bomb fell a hundred metres away, she was showered with a light spray of damp sand which smelt not of salt and seaweed but high explosive.

Finally the aircraft disappeared. Turpin came running over the beach. Wisps of smoke from the fresh bomb craters drifted into the air like miniature volcanoes, mixing with that of the campfires. Here and there, fragments of uniforms and burning rubber smouldered. He weaved between the knots of soldiers. Some were groaning, some wept or uttered stifled screams; most swore quietly under their breath or sat in numbed silence. He stopped by a bedraggled group of gunners and stared around like a madman on the run.

'Bess!' he yelled. 'Bess! Bess! Where are you, Bess?'

'There's no Bess round here, mate!' one of the gunners called to him. 'You know anyone called Bess?' he asked his comrades. They all shook their heads.

Turpin gaped at them, then ran on.

'Poor mucker!' one of the gunners said as Turpin disappeared. 'He's got shell shock and has lost his marbles.'

'Bess!' Turpin called again. 'Bess! Bess! Where's my Bess?'

She was nowhere. He halted to get his bearings. He was too far along the beach, too near the trees. Yet everywhere looked the same, the hunched gatherings of men, the drifting smoke, the grey forbidding sea beyond them.

Turning, he ran back along the beach. Jet heard him coming and sat up, a fine covering of sand on her black coat.

Still not seeing her, Turpin again shouted out her name.

For the first time in weeks, Jet let out a single, sharp bark. Turpin heard it and swung round to see her head and shoulders above the edge of their trench. He ran towards her and threw himself down next to her, cradling her head and stroking her, dusting the sand off her.

'Bess,' he almost whispered. 'I thought they'd got you. But you're fine, just fine.' To reassure himself, he quickly checked her over. She was unscathed.

At his touch, Jet put her forepaws on the edge of the trench and, lifting herself up, licked Turpin's face. His rough stubble was coarse upon her tongue. Her tail whipped little bursts of sand into the air. Turpin hugged her then, tears running down his cheeks and mixing with the wet smears of her tongue on his chin.

Towards the late afternoon, vessels began to appear off-shore. A few were grey warships, but the rest were a strange assortment of craft – lifeboats and fishing smacks, luxury cruisers and weekend fishing boats, even paddle-steamers and a tug towing a line of four coal barges. The soldiers, seeing the ships arriving, formed long lines snaking out into the sea. Those at the head of these long queues of men waiting to be rescued stood in the sea up to their armpits, holding their kit and rifles – if they still had them – over their heads.

Turpin and Jet abandoned their trench and joined one of the lines. It was already at least two hundred metres long.

'Just like the Cup Final at Wembley,' quipped a cor-poral as they walked up to stand behind him.

'Yes,' Turpin answered, adding, 'do you think we'll get in before the match kicks off?'

'No way of telling, mate,' the corporal replied. 'They're working the turnstile so slow we might not even get to see the final whistle.'

The two soldiers looked at each other. They might have been talking about football, yet they knew what they really meant. It would be a miracle if even half of the thousands of men lining up patiently to be rescued off the beach, were ever to see England again.

'This your mutt?' the corporal enquired, eager to change the subject and nodding at Jet.

'My Bess,' replied Turpin.

'Where did you pick it up? One of my platoon found — you won't believe this, mate! — a monkey. Not far from Ypres. In a house. Jerry'd shot the place up, the owners had scarpered, the monkey was left chained to a perch like a parrot. The boy wondered if it would understand him. I mean, the monkey must speak French or something, mustn't it?' He patted Jet briefly. 'Your mutt will have to parley English when it gets over the channel.'

'I didn't pick her up,' Turpin explained. 'She speaks English already. She's . . .'

He suddenly felt terribly tired. The months of fighting, of working his way towards Germany and then being beaten back were beginning to tell.

'I'm her handler,' he said simply.

They did not speak again. Instead, they faced the sea as the night fell, and the ships and boats and little craft moved offshore to avoid being stranded by the waning tide. Once it was dark, the lines broke up, the troops moving higher up the beach where the sand was dry.

Turpin dug another trench. He lay down in it, Jet snuggling close to him. Neither really slept; a cold breeze started to come off the sea and their shallow trench provided little protection. At midnight they split a dried biscuit between them, washing the crumbs down with sips of water.

'If fortune doesn't smile on us tomorrow, Bess,' Turpin said quietly, 'if we don't get on a boat, we're scuppered. That's the last of our scoff and we've only half the canteen left of water.'

As daylight broke, the lines formed again. The smaller vessels began to return inshore to ferry the men out to the larger craft which could not come in close: the beach shelved gradually for some way out. By chance, Turpin joined one of the shortest queues and found himself standing ankle-deep in the sea, with Jet beside him.

The water fascinated her. It had a strange smell to it. Little waves lapped against her legs, tickling her fur. Minute fish darted about. She pricked her ears at them, watching them flick to and fro, tiny silver flashes in the early light. When she felt thirsty, she bent her head to drink: the water tasted foul and she puckered her nose.

Very gradually, the queue advanced and the tide rose. It was not long before Turpin was standing up to his shins in the sea and Jet was in it up to her belly. The smaller waves, which had previously tickled her, now flicked salt spray into her nose and eyes. She had to blink and shake her head every few minutes to clear her nostrils of the stinging.

Two cabin cruisers were serving the queue, ferrying the men out to a paddle-steamer called *The Medway Queen* which was riding at anchor a few hundred metres offshore. Being only about four metres long, each boat could take no more than eight men at a time. Turpin reckoned there were about three hundred men in the line in front of them and that each journey to the paddle-steamer and back took each boat twenty-one minutes. At that rate, he guessed it would be about noon when he and Jet reached the head of the line. He wondered if the tide would be out then, forcing the boats away from the beach, but guessed it would not matter. The line of men would simply walk further into the sea.

At nine o'clock, German fighter bombers flew over. They ignored the men on the beaches and concentrated on the rescue fleet. The warships opened fire on them. When one aircraft was hit and plunged into the sea with an explosion, the soldiers cheered. Yet most of the aircraft escaped and at least a dozen little boats were lost.

Half an hour later, fighters returned and strafed the beaches. Everyone threw themselves down on the sand. Those in the sea could do nothing but stand and hope they were not hit. The air misted with the grim, grey smoke of high explosives, a haze of sand drifting on the stiff breeze.

In the line, a few of the soldiers swore or shook their fists at the enemy aircraft, yet most were silent. They just stared ahead out to sea, praying hard their little cabin cruisers were not destroyed. Everyone knew that if the boats were lost, then so would they be.

As the queue edged forwards and the sea got deeper, it became impossible for Jet to stand, so Turpin picked her up, at first holding her under his arm so she half floated.

'I'd let it go, if I was you,' advised a sergeant standing behind them. 'Let the dog loose on the beach, take its chances. It'll survive. You go on up, I'll save your place here for you.'

'I'll keep her with me,' Turpin replied. 'We've been through a lot.'

'It'll hamper you,' the sergeant said. 'Once you get into deeper water, it'll start to tire you. Then you'll both be done for.'

'I'll risk it,' Turpin declared stolidly and he faced the sea again.

By half-past eleven, they were only twenty-five from the front of the queue. Turpin was up to his chest in the sea, his uniform shiny from the oil which floated on the surface, spewed from craft which had been sunk. Like his uniform, Jet's fur was matted with oil. He made sure she did not try to lick herself clean. The oil would be sure to poison her.

No longer able to fit under Turpin's arm, Jet was draped about his shoulders, her feet down either side of his face.

'If that was a manky dead fox,' remarked a private in front of them, 'and you had a sour grin on your face like you'd just sucked a lemon, you'd look just like my wife's mother.'

No sooner had he spoken than the drone of aircraft filled the sky. Turpin could not look up for Jet's bulk prevented him from turning his head: yet the private could. He glanced along the beach, then stared.

'The bastards!' he suddenly bellowed. 'They're strafing the lines in the sea!'

The drone rose to an ear-shattering crescendo. The very air seemed to vibrate. Around the line, the water spat and jumped and hissed as if it had suddenly come to the boil. The sergeant behind Turpin howled briefly; there was a splash and he was silent. Turpin strained to look over Jet's back, and caught a glimpse of the sergeant's body drifting away just under the surface, a pinkish cloud spreading out from his chest. The private crossed himself and closed his eyes.

The aircraft wheeled in the sky and angled for a return run.

'They're coming back!' someone yelled needlessly.

This time, they flew lower, faster. Turpin could see the guns mounted in their wings sparking. In the sky around the aircraft appeared little puffballs of smoke as the anti-aircraft gunners on the warships brought their sights to bear. A parallel row of little water spouts raced towards the queue.

Tiny whistling sounds filled Jet's ears. A searing pain cut through Turpin's shoulder. Jet let out a yelp and began to thrash about. It was all he could do to keep her in place. He had to fight to maintain his balance. Both Jet's struggling and the impact of the shell fragment almost knocked him over.

'It's all right, Bess!' he muttered. 'Good girl! Good girl!'

He reached up to stroke her. A vicious pain stabbed through to the centre of his back. His hand and voice calmed her but as soon as his fingers touched her he felt the slick, slimy warmth of blood.

Jet tried not to wriggle but the pain was intense, made worse by the salt water. She wanted desperately – instinctively – to lick her wound but she could not get at it.

'You got hit,' the private commented unnecessarily as the fighters veered away inland, chased by more puffballs. 'Let me take a gander at it.' He felt about Turpin's shoulder and said, 'You've got a bit of shrapnel in your shoulder. Made a bit of a mess . . .'

'The hell with that!' Turpin exclaimed. 'What about my dog?'

The private examined Jet. His hands were soft, searching, soothing.

'She's got a fragment, too. Just behind her neck. Bleeding a lot. I'll see what I can do.'

He fumbled about under his helmet and produced a mustard-yellow woollen scarf from which he tore a length.

'Made by my wife's mother,' he said. 'What a colour! Looks like cat's vomit.'

He rolled the piece up and pressed it into Jet's wound, shifting her harness to hold it in place.

'Best I can do, pal. It'll staunch the bleeding a bit.'

For half an hour, Turpin strove to keep his balance. The pain was fast sapping his strength and he began to feel light-headed. The water around him was as pink as it had been around the dead sergeant. Twice, he began to stumble but the private held him up, slapping his face to keep his attention and saying, 'Hold on, chum! Hold on! The boat'll be here in a tick.'

Jet kept as still as she could. Her injury throbbed with every beat of her heart and the smell of her own blood disturbed her. Like her master, she was beginning to feel a little faint from the shock and loss of blood.

At last, the cabin cruiser was alongside them. Willing hands reached over the gunwales, removing her from Turpin's shoulders. She was put in the cabin, on a leather seat much stained with salt and oil. Turpin, now unconscious, was carried in and laid next to her. The private sat down and checked Jet's makeshift bandage.

'We'll soon have you safe and sound on the transport,' he said as he repositioned her harness. 'Twenty minutes to a hot dish of Bovril for you and a cuppa for me. What do you say to that, doggie?'

Jet feebly wagged her tail and rested her head on Turpin's chest.

'Look!' said the corporal, who was leaning against the polished wood of the bulkhead beside Turpin, and smoking a bent Woodbine.

Turpin tried to sit up but could not; his back seemed somehow fixed to the canvas of the stretcher.

'What is it?' he asked with a hoarse croak.

'Wonderful!' the corporal replied, as he took the cigarette out of his mouth and held it to Turpin's lips. 'More grey than white, mind. But with a green line on the top.'

'What?' Turpin asked again.

'The white cliffs of Dover,' the corporal replied. 'We're nearly home, pal.'

Turpin let his hand creep along the deck. Jet was still

lying next to him. She was cold and wet from the spray off the paddle wheels. The blood on her shoulder had congealed into a hard mat with her fur. With difficulty, Turpin turned his head to look at her.

'You hear that, Bess? We're nearly home.'

Half an hour later, Turpin was carried down the gangplank on to the quay at Dover, Jet limping by the side of one of the stretcher bearers. Her shoulder was still viciously painful and, with each step, something seemed to pierce her muscle like a hot needle. She did not whimper, however, but stoically tried to keep up with the stretcher as it was carried towards a waiting ambulance. As the medical orderlies slid Turpin into the ambulance, she tried to climb through the door.

'This your dog?' one of the orderlies asked. 'You Tommies! I don't know. You come through hell with your pet dog. You should have left it over there, chum.'

'She's not my pet,' Turpin whispered hoarsely. 'She's an infantry patrol dog. I'm her handler.'

'Right!' the orderly said then, turning, shouted, 'Quartermaster!'

A warrant officer came quickly over, a sheaf of papers under his arm and a row of pencils in his pocket. He looked harassed and tired.

'The dog's an army beast,' the orderly said. 'Injured,' he added.

'Fine!' the quartermaster replied, then shouted over his shoulder, 'Williams, find me some rope, PDQ.'

The ambulance engine started up, a puff of black smoke pumping from its exhaust pipe. The medical orderly closed one of the ambulance doors. A lance corporal approached with a length of rope and spoke to the quartermaster.

'Her name's Bess,' Turpin called out as loudly as he could over the sound of the closing door and motor.

'What's that?' the quartermaster replied, half-turning.

'My dog. Her name's Bess,' Turpin answered as loudly as he could, the strain hurting his lungs.

The quartermaster nodded. The medical orderly slammed shut the second ambulance door as the lance corporal threaded the rope through Jet's harness. Leaning over, the quartermaster cursorily studied Jet's ear, taking a pencil out of his pocket and licking the lead.

'QM!' someone called out urgently. 'Over here, sir. Got a bit of a problem. What do we do with a box of Jerry grenades?'

Distracted for a moment, the quartermaster shouted back, 'I'll be right over,' and quickly scribbled down on a sheet of paper *Dog D67: Name – Jess*.

The ambulance revved up and drove away leaving Jet standing with the lance-corporal. She was never to see Turpin again.

The huge studded door to Dorchester Prison swung open. Although it was drizzling, Fred blinked as if he was coming out of a darkened room into brilliant sunlight. He stretched, picked up his bag and set off towards the railway station.

It was prepared for war. The windows were hung with blackout curtains and the entrance was sandbagged. The ticket clerk carried a gas mask in a small cardboard box around his neck. Upon a notice-board next to the time-table was a gaudy poster with a cartoon of two sailors talking over a table under which Hitler was hiding: the caption read *Tittle Tattle Lost The Battle*. Purchasing a single ticket, Fred boarded the train waiting at the platform. As he settled himself back into his seat, the locomotive blew a blast on its whistle and pumped smoke from its funnel.

At Crayham, he alighted from the train and made his way straight to the police station. He walked in and up to the charge desk. The constable seated behind it looked hardly older than a boy.

'I'd like to see Sergeant Cobb, please,' Fred requested.

'He's not here, not any more. He's in Portsmouth, training air raid wardens.'

Fred, somewhat taken aback, said, 'My name's Parry. Alfred Parry.'

The constable thought for a moment, then replied, 'Oh, yes. Mr Parry. The sergeant thought you'd be round. He left this for you.'

The constable opened a drawer and removed an envelope which he handed to Fred. He sat down opposite the desk and tore it open. Inside was a brief letter.

Dear Fred, he read, *I kept my promise and saw Jet was not destroyed. However, no one in Crayham would take her on, so she was requisitioned by the army. She was taken for training and that is all I know. You will not, I'm afraid, be able to reclaim her or even visit her. Indeed, there is no way of telling — with the war on — where she is or what has or will become of her. I'm sorry my news is not what you would want to hear. We must, alas, all make sacrifices at this terrible time. Yours sincerely, Jim Cobb.*

Fred sat back and stared at the wall. He could feel hot tears welling into his eyes and he pinched his nose to stop them coming.

'Not bad news, I hope, sir?' the constable enquired.

Making no reply, Fred folded the letter and put it in his pocket. Picking up his bag, he walked out of the police station and down the High Street until he came to a building which, before the war, had been the church hall. Outside on a board was stuck the second poster he consciously read that day. This was no cartoon. It showed a painting of Britannia standing with her spear and shield, upon which was emblazoned the Union Jack. *England Expects*, the text read, *National Service*.

Fred entered the building. At the end of the hall stood a table behind which an elderly man with a wide, waxed ginger moustache was writing on a pad of notepaper. As Fred approached, the man put down his pen and looked up.

'Can I help you, son?' he asked in a kindly voice.

'Yes,' Fred answered. 'I've come to join up.'

The man smiled and pulled a form out of a tray, the paper rustling like burning leaves.

'That's a fine thing to do, son,' he said softly. 'After Dunkirk, we need young men like you. Just fill out the details and sign at the bottom, if you will.'

'Eyes – *right!*' the regimental sergeant–major bellowed. 'About – *TURN!*' The second word sounded more like a strangulated scream than a word. 'Halt! Stand at *EASE!* Stand easy!'

The squad relaxed, some of the privates panting from exertion.

'Pay attention!' the RSM shouted. 'All you green and sickly monkeys – weapons training, lecture 1. Barrack 4. *MOVE!*'

Everyone set off at the run, heading for Barrack 4. Fred was the first to arrive. Despite his months in prison, he was still fit from his life as a poacher. He sat on a bench in the front row. Before him stood a warrant officer holding a

Lee Enfield .303 rifle. As soon as the rest of the squad were seated, the warrant officer began his lecture.

'First off, we have naming of parts,' he started, pointing to various bits of the gun as he spoke. 'This is the lower swing swivel and this is the upper sling swivel and this is the piling swivel which you won't get on your weapons. This is the safety catch, this the trigger guard, this the trigger. Foresight, back-sight. Bolt . . .'

Outside, a lorry pulled up with a grinding of gears. A voice called out a command Fred could not quite comprehend, which was followed by the rattle of chains as the rear board of the vehicle was lowered. Then, quite distinctly, he could hear dogs barking. There was a window at the end of the bench but the sill was too high. Fred could see nothing through it except the roof of the lorry cab.

'. . . Breech, barrel. Finally, the butt. Now,' the warrant officer stopped and looked around the room, his eye falling on Fred, 'perhaps the prat in the front row who wants to go out and play with the doggies might tell me what this –' he pointed to a box-like piece under the breech '– is.'

For a moment, Fred was back in the countryside around Crayham, Jet at his heel and a new moon high in the sky.

'*YOU!*' the warrant officer bawled.

Fred's attention was snapped back to the present.

'What is this, you gormless oik?'

'Magazine, sir,' Fred said: he knew the parts of a rifle off by heart. He had used one often enough.

'Right!' the warrant officer answered, a little surprised. 'Just you be sure you don't wander off again.'

After the lecture, the squad were stood down. Fred saunt-
ered across to the driver of the lorry, who was sitting on
the bumper smoking a cigarette.

'Hello,' Fred said, 'you didn't happen to have a black
Lab cross bitch on your vehicle this morning?'

'No, mate. All sorts but no Labs.'

'Have you seen one?' Fred asked.

'Have I seen one?' the driver repeated. 'You trying to be
funny? Since the war started, I've seen hundreds.' He
flicked his cigarette under a wheel. 'Push off, will you! I've
no time for jokers.' And, with that, he started up the lorry
and drove off.

PART TWO

NOVEMBER 1940–SEPTEMBER 1942

After her evacuation from Dunkirk, Jet was held for six months in a veterinary kennels. While the private's scarf had saved her life by preventing her from bleeding to death, it had introduced an infection into the wound which, with the oil and salt from the sea, had slowed healing. For the first weeks, she spent most of her time lying in the sunshine in her run, occasionally trying to tug at the tight bandages.

The officer in charge of the kennels was Major Allsop, an elderly man called back into service when the war began. He frequently visited her, changing her bandages and making a fuss of her: yet he was not Turpin. Jet missed him, the reassurance of his voice and his smell, his close warmth in a bivouac or trench, the steadying touch of his hand when on patrol.

Once she began to move again, the muscles in her shoulder starting to knit, Jet discovered she was not the only wounded dog in the kennels. Next to her run was an Irish terrier who had lost an ear at the fall of Calais and, beyond that, a collie with only one hind leg who had been blown up by a mine.

After three months, Jet was taken for daily exercise to a large field where Major Allsop trotted her round the perimeter. Then he took her through her commands to ensure she did not forget them; not that there was much worry of that happening for such skills were embedded in her mind.

In the last week of November, Jet was woken one morning by Major Allsop rattling her leash. As he unbolted her kennel, he said, 'Come along, Jess. You're discharged from sick bay and back on active service.'

She was led out to a van and, on the order, jumped into the rear to discover the interior reeked of the most delicious but faint aroma of meat, bones and suet. Along the roof hung several rails with hooks dangling from them, while, to one side, were scrubbed wooden shelves. Had she been able to read, she would have seen, still visible under the coat of army khaki paint on the van, the letters *C. W. Moss – Family Butchers – founded 1902*. Like her, the vehicle had been requisitioned. Lying on a layer of clean hay, she settled down for what was to be a long journey. Twice the van stopped, Allsop appearing with a bowl of water, then taking her for a short walk.

In the mid-afternoon, they arrived at a small barracks. The buildings were made of red brick under grey slate roofs which shone with the light rain. Jet was led through a door and taken to a room in which there was a desk, several chairs, a wooden filing cabinet and a black telephone which pinged every so often, catching her attention. Another elderly officer entered and he and Major Allsop shook hands.

'Hello, Alan. This your Dunkirk survivor?'

'This is the one. D67. The last handler apparently called her Jess.'

The officer picked up a manila dossier and opening it said, 'Not a very fat record. Hardly anything here.'

'Her original papers are mislaid. Believed lost in that air raid last month on — well, you know what I'm referring to,' Major Allsop replied. 'Jerry's bombers hit that target fair and square. Anyway,' he went on, 'all we've got now dates back only to her return from Dunkirk.'

The officer lifted the few sheets of paper in the folder. 'According to her last handler, who was interviewed about her in hospital, the bitch was A1 in basic training. He also received her well-trained, it seems. A very intelligent dog, he said, and an excellent infantry patrol animal. She should adapt well.'

'Going by his comments,' Major Allsop remarked, 'she'll not need much attention. Who's she going to?'

The elderly officer studied the dossier and answered, 'Sergeant Ken Hogan. He was regular army, went into the reserves but now he's called up and going to be attached to either a field medical unit or to civil defence. Do you want to take her along? He's waiting at the end of the corridor, Room 133.'

Major Allsop signed a sheet of paper and led Jet out of the office and down a long passageway which smelt of polish. Her newly-trimmed claws clicked on the wooden floorboards. In Room 133 stood a man about thirty-five years old. He wore a military uniform, but instead of a revolver or pack he carried a gas mask case attached to his belt.

He saluted Major Allsop, then, squatting down until his face was nearly level with Jet's, said, 'So you're my new little charmer, are you?'

He rubbed his fist behind Jet's right ear: it was just as if she was scratching it herself and she felt her hind leg want to join in.

'D67. She answers to Jess,' Major Allsop explained. 'She won't run very well.'

'So I understand, sir,' Sergeant Hogan said as he ran his hand over Jet's shoulder. 'I can feel the scar, sir. Any bone damage?'

'None. A shell fragment lodged in the muscle. She was lucky – far luckier than her handler. He'll not be called up again, poor chap. I hope you've better fortune with her, sergeant.'

Accepting her leash, Sergeant Hogan saluted again and took Jet outside and down some steps, to where a shining black Norton motorcycle and side-car combination was parked.

'Might as well make the most of an official petrol ration,' he told her as he lifted her into the side-car, clipping a short leash on to her harness. 'Better to give the old machine an airing than ride in a stuffy car. I'll bet you've had enough of that for one day. What a torture that must have been. A butcher's van to transport a dog! Trust the army . . .'

He swung his leg over the motorbike, turned the ignition key and snapped his foot down on the starting pedal. The engine spluttered into life.

Tugging a pair of goggles over his eyes, Hogan let the clutch lever out. The motorbike moved away from the steps, accelerated across the parade ground, drove past the sentry box and out through the gate on to the main road. The rain had given way to weak autumnal sunshine, the air chill but not too cold despite the approach of the early darkness.

Jet thoroughly enjoyed the ride. She had never been in a side-car before and sat bolt upright, looking ahead over a small and ineffectual windscreen. The wind flapped her ears, her eyes streamed with tears, and her mouth, when she opened it, was filled with a blast of air which took her breath away – yet she was excited. As they drove down a street full of shops, people turned and stared at her, pointing and gesticulating. A little girl waved to her. A Pekinese, attached by a white leather lead to a dumpy woman in a fur coat, yapped furiously at the sight.

The motorcycle left the town and, after ten minutes of swerving along a country lane, with Jet leaning this way and that to keep her balance, slowed down and pulled into a cobbled yard between a paddock and a cottage. By now, it was dark and no lights showed from the cottage at all. Every window was covered by thick black-out curtains.

Hogan turned into a barn, switched off the engine, removed his goggles and hung them from the handlebars and, swinging himself off the saddle, unclipped Jet's harness.

'Come along then, Jess my girl!' he exclaimed. 'Time you met the Hogan tribe. Heel!'

Jet walked by his side towards the cottage. Hogan opened a door from which a weak light filtered out. Entering a kitchen, she was suddenly encased in a homely perfume of humans, wood smoke and roasting meat, all slightly tinged with cat. From the roof beams hung copper pots and pans. A Welsh dresser against one wall was lined with rows of plates. The faint light came from a huge, black iron stove.

'I'm back!' Hogan called out as he closed the door, switching on a light and hanging Jet's lead on a hook.

Jet listened. She could hear footsteps approaching across a flag-stoned floor. An old wooden door creaked on its hinges to show a slim, pretty woman wearing a jumper, a flowered dress and an apron.

'Hello, Ken,' Mrs Hogan said, 'I didn't hear you drive up.' She kissed her husband on the cheek, then looked at Jet. 'My word! But you *are* a pretty dog!' she exclaimed.

Jet wagged her tail, opening her mouth slightly in a pant of greeting. Just the woman's tone of voice in those few words told her this was going to be a friendly, peaceful place.

'Have you got her, Pa?' a voice called, quickly followed by another asking, 'Have you brought her home, Pa?'

Two girls, aged ten and twelve, appeared in the doorway. Both of them were wearing flannelette nightdresses.

'Well, Jess,' Hogan said, bending down to Jet, 'now you see them all. Mrs Hogan, Phillie – that's the one with bunches – and Cassie. Everybody, this is Jess. She's not a

68

pet, mind. She's a working dog and I've got to train her. But she'll live with us. She's already had her share of fighting Jerry. She was taken off the beaches at Dunkirk.'

'She's gorgeous!' exclaimed Cassie.

'Can we stroke her?' Phillie enquired.

'Yes. She's a good-natured dog. I can tell that much from her. But don't touch her left shoulder, just in case. She had a nasty wound there.'

The two girls approached Jet, who let them run their hands over her back and head. Then Cassie put her face down right next to Jet's and said softly, 'Do you give kisses, Jess?'

Jet opened her mouth and ran her tongue right up the girl's cheek. It tasted of soap.

A movement caught Jet's eye. In the doorway stood a tabby tomcat, its fur striped with white markings on its chest and front paws. It did not arch its back and hiss but surveyed the kitchen with a typical feline aloofness.

'Oh, dear!' muttered Mrs Hogan apprehensively. 'I had hoped to introduce them gradually.'

'This,' Hogan said to Jet, 'is Benjy.'

Jet watched the cat cautiously. She knew how it could turn from being a placid, dozy animal to a spitting, clawing demon in less than a second; in her mind, she would rather face a weasel in a woodshed than a cat in a kitchen. This cottage might not turn out to be such a friendly, peaceful place as she had thought. After a long pause, Benjy stepped lazily towards Jet who kept her head high. Cats, she knew, could do painful things to soft noses. Drawing close to Jet, the cat sniffed at her mouth and then, much to Jet's astonishment, rubbed itself against her front legs and sat down to wash itself with a detached air of nonchalance.

'Well, I'll be!' Hogan burst out. 'Old Benjy must know there's a war on and that he has to make sacrifices, too.'

That night, Jet lay in a wicker basket next to the stove, a blanket folded under her. Benjy curled up on a cushion on a chair by the table. As she fell asleep, the room lit by flames flickering behind the stove door, Jet found herself half remembering another cottage and another stove. It had all been long ago; and that room had smelled not so much of cat as hanging pheasants and paunched hares.

Within an hour of Jet's first training session with Hogan, he knew he had a superlative dog. She was utterly obedient to all commands and proved to be highly intelligent. What was more, she could hold her attention for long spans and was not easily distracted. Indeed, the only drawback he could see in her performance was that she was unable to run quickly. Her muscles were still stiff from her wound.

'Never you mind, Jess,' he said to her at the end of their first morning working together. 'The job you're doing for the time being isn't going to involve running after Jerry.'

At mid-day, Hogan took Jess in the side-car to a pub where the landlady made a huge fuss of her, providing her with a tin bowl of milky water. To every customer who entered she announced, 'This is Ken's new dog, Jess. She's a hero of Dunkirk.' At this, everyone patted Jet or stroked her, some slipping her a crust of bread or a sliver of cheese when Hogan's back was turned. By two o'clock, she felt ready to have a doze but it was not to be; they went back to the barracks and out on to an assault and battle course. There they met six privates standing in a group chatting by a semi-derelict wooden hut. As Hogan approached, they smartened themselves up, stubbing out their cigarettes with their boots and forming a ragged line.

'Afternoon, lads!' Hogan greeted them somewhat inappropriately. They were none of them young, being clearly men who had joined up over the age limit for active service yet were keen to serve their country: one of them was at least ten years older than Hogan. 'This is Jess, our new casualty hunter,' he continued. 'Now you know what you're here for, don't you?'

The privates nodded, one of them adding, 'We're all on our last legs, sir. Bought it. Injured and in need of rescue, sir.'

'That's about the sum of it,' Hogan confirmed. 'We'll start off with just two of you. Deacon, Wintle – go and injure yourselves. The rest of you stand easy.'

Two of the men disappeared around the hut whilst the rest sat down on a low brick wall. Hogan waited a few minutes, then took Jet behind the hut. In front of her stretched what looked like a battlefield. There were ditches filled with stagnant water, several derelict buildings, a high wall strewn with ropes, some fallen tree trunks, a fifty-metre length of tangled and rusting barbed wire and a pond with a makeshift plank bridge across it.

Hogan bent to Jet, removing her leash from her harness.

'Seek!' he ordered her.

Jet knew what to do. Somewhere in the course in front

of her were men whom she had to locate. She set off, moving quickly despite her tugging muscles. It was only a matter of a minute before she traced the first private who was hiding in one of the ruined buildings. She located his position, sat down and glanced over her shoulder.

Hogan smiled and walked up to her.

'Good girl, Jess,' he praised her, clipping on her leash. 'Come!'

Much to her consternation, he led her right into the building and up to the private, who was lying still with his eyes shut amidst a rubble of stones. Hogan encouraged Jet to nuzzle him, upon which the private opened his eyes and moaned realistically. Then, reaching into his pocket, Hogan took out a dog biscuit and gave it to her. When the same thing happened again with the second private, who was prone behind one of the tree trunks, Jet got the idea: she was not just to locate the men but actually go up to them.

For three weeks, Hogan took her through her training. Sometimes the same privates arrived: sometimes it was others. At one session, it was not soldiers at all, but a group of women and children who feigned injury; Jet considered they were far more effective actors than the soldiers. Some of the training days were harder than others. Once Jet was fully aware of her task, other factors were introduced. She had to work her way through the assault course whilst under fire from thunderflash grenades, small-arms fire and timed explosions, which sprayed her with mud. She did not flinch once. She had been through all this already.

'Marvellous how calm she is,' Major Allsop remarked,

visiting to view her progress. 'You'd think after Dunkirk she'd jump at a Christmas cracker.'

'She's a remarkable dog, sir,' Hogan agreed. 'I don't think I've ever seen the likes of her. Dedicated, set in her mind and quick to learn. If my daughters took to their mathematics that fast . . . Well, they'd be professors at Oxford University by now.'

'How is she at home?'

'Family pet, sir. I couldn't ask for better. Even leaves the cat alone. But once we're out of the house, she's ready for business.'

'Well,' Major Allsop informed him, 'you're going into business from next week – but not in the battlefield. You're being posted to a civil defence unit. Can't tell you which city. Walls have ears. But you know as well as I do the Luftwaffe is giving us a pounding. It's no secret many of our major towns and cities are being bombed almost nightly.'

Hogan was silent for a minute, then said, 'I'm not worried where I go, sir. Just so long as I'm doing my bit. And I'll bet, if she could talk, Jess would agree.'

Major Allsop touched Hogan on his sleeve, saying, 'You're a good man, Hogan. And with that dog you'll be a damned fine team.'

'A tiny favour if I may, sir?' Hogan asked as he, Jet and the major walked away from the battle course. 'I'd like to keep Jess with me, sir. Not have her housed in a kennels. We've grown close, I'd say, sir . . .'

'No worry about that,' Major Allsop replied. 'You'll be billeted in Civvy Street, not in a barracks, so the dog will be with you at all times. Besides, she'll have to be. You'll be on call twenty-four hours a day.'

The Victorian brick house to which Hogan and Jet moved was at the end of a terrace on the outskirts of a small industrial sea port. The front door gave directly on to the pavement down three stone steps, which the owner, a widow called Mrs Hartop, scrupulously polished every Monday morning just after doing her weekly wash.

At the start, she was not at all sure of Jet. The first time she saw her, her reaction was, 'I don't really like dogs. See, when I was a little girl, a big brute attacked me and bit me. Right here!' at which words she lifted her skirt and rolled down her thick stocking to display an ancient scar on her calf.

'I can assure you my Jess won't do anything like that!' Hogan remarked. 'She's as gentle as a kitten.'

'That's what they said about Rex,' Mrs Hartop retorted balefully. 'And he was the one what bit me.' She sighed and looked at Jet sitting obediently at Hogan's side. 'Still, there's a war on and we have to accept these things. At least,' she went on, 'you're a gentleman and it could be worse. I could have some evacuee children. Little terrors they can be, I can tell you.' She nodded her head knowingly and winked ominously. 'I know people in the countryside what's got them.'

Hogan and Jet shared the back upstairs bedroom. It was sparsely furnished with a single bed with a lumpy mattress, a chair, a dressing table with a mirror and a small wardrobe, whose door had to be kept shut with a wedge of cardboard. Beside the window, criss-crossed with gummed brown paper strips, hung a heavy blackout curtain. It overlooked the narrow garden in which there was a minute square of grass, a flowerbed full of weeds and a flagged pathway, leading to a shed and an outside toilet.

'Well, here we are,' Hogan said to Jet as he dropped his kit bag on the bed. 'Home away from home. I'll have the bed and you can have the corner by the dresser.' He put the blanket from her basket on the floor, placing her water bowl next to it. 'Whatever you do,' he continued with a smile, 'don't slurp water on the floorboards. I don't think her downstairs would approve.' He nodded at his feet and, lowering his voice, said, 'I think we'd best get well in with her. We're here for a few months.'

At night fall on their first evening, they went downstairs to Mrs Hartop's back parlour where she was cooking their evening meal of shepherd's pie and broad beans. They were to discover shepherd's pie was served at least three times a week because she had a nephew who lived in the nearby hills where he kept sheep and grew potatoes. The alternative was rabbit stew, from the same source. Jet preferred the smell of the latter; it had a familiarity which she somehow recognised.

'That was excellent,' Hogan said as he mopped up the last of his gravy with a crust of bread. 'Mustn't waste a bit, and not just because of the war-time shortages.' He pushed away his empty plate. 'That was as good as my wife's and that's no lie.'

Mrs Hartop smiled at his compliment, left the table and sat in an easy chair. She switched the radio on, the volume low. A dance band was playing, the tunes interspersed by the bandleader announcing the next, or introducing a singer. Jet lay curled before a small gas fire which hissed in a tiled fireplace.

'Take the other chair,' she invited Hogan. 'That was Mr Hartop's,' she added with a hint of reverence. 'You've been called up, have you?'

'I was in the reserves,' Hogan replied as he lowered himself into the old armchair which smelt of leather and sweet pipe tobacco. 'When the going got tough after Dunkirk, I was recalled. I'm a bit long in the tooth now, but the way things are everyone has to pull together.'

'This your dog, then?' she enquired, adding as a reminder, 'I don't like dogs myself.'

'In a manner of speaking. She's not my pet. She's an army dog. I'm her handler and trained her. Well, to tell the truth, she was already well-trained. I just taught her a few new tricks.'

'She's a bit lame for a military animal,' Mrs Hartop observed, as Jet stood up to walk round in a tight circle before awkwardly settling herself once more. 'She can't be much use.'

Hogan then recounted Jet's story, her patrolling behind enemy lines and her escape from Dunkirk. He made up most of the story from his imagination, based on the little he knew of Jet's experiences so far in the war. The way he told it, however, it made a good yarn and, as he talked, he could see Mrs Hartop looking more and more at Jet. By the time he was finished, he was sure she was a changed person – and he was right.

'Well, I never!' Mrs Hartop exclaimed. 'To think that poor dog's been through all that. And now it's lying on my hearth as snug as a bug in a rug!' She cautiously reached over the edge of her chair. 'Do you think . . .?' she began.

'I'm sure,' Hogan replied, smiling.

Mrs Hartop let her fingers just graze the top of Jet's head. She opened her eyes, gazing up with the dreamy look dogs have when they are warm, comfortable and only half awake. Mrs Hartop withdrew her hand. Jet sensed the faint smell of fear coming off her skin.

'You'll be on duty tonight?' Mrs Hartop asked.

Hogan glanced at his watch and said, 'I'll be off in five minutes. Have to be at the area civil defence headquarters by half past.'

'Let's hope you have a quiet night. For all our sakes,' she commented with some feeling. Then, dipping a spoon in the shepherd's pie bowl, she scraped out the remains and tentatively held them out for Jet, saying, 'You don't mind, do you?'

Jet, scenting the food on offer near her nose, sat up but did not take it. She was trained not to accept food from strangers.

'Go on, Jess,' Hogan ordered.

Jet stood and licked the spoon spotlessly clean in less than thirty seconds.

The streets were still. Not a light shone. All the street-lamps had been switched off and not a single, narrow ray of light escaped from a house. Everyone knew to show no lights. The smallest beam eking out of a window, slipping past a carelessly hung black-out curtain, could be the one clue a German bomber pilot flying high above needed in order to pinpoint his target.

Not only were the streets dark, they were uncannily silent. No cars drove by. No one cycled past with a cheery wave or a mumbled 'Evening!' No one made their way home from the pub or the cinema, the church hall or a friend's house.

'Like a ghost town,' Hogan remarked to Jet as they made their way along a street of terraced houses. 'You wouldn't think thirty-thousand people lived within a two-mile radius of where we're walking.'

He briefly shone his torch ahead down the pavement. It was a specially adapted torch with a cowl which ensured the light could only shine downwards. A cat jumped off a wall, ran across the street and disappeared down an alley.

'At least something's stirring,' Hogan continued. 'It's uncanny otherwise.'

For Jet, it was not a silent street. Her hearing being much sharper than Hogan's, she could pick up the sounds of radios giving out the late evening news, babies crying, kettles whistling on the boil, people talking, water running into tubs, cats miaowing and, by a park, bats clicking in the night sky.

'Just as well there's no moon,' Hogan said, as they reached the end of the park where the railings had recently been removed, the metal carted off for use in the manufacture of weapons. 'When they can see by moonlight – that's when the bombers come.' He glanced up. 'Too much cloud tonight. But you wait, my girl. Another few days, when the moon's up and the weather's clearer . . . We'll be busy enough then. Busy sorting out the devil's work for him.'

They halted under a large oak tree, Hogan removing a map from his pocket. On the order, Jet sat whilst Hogan studied the street plan with his torch.

'Now there's the park,' he said to himself, 'and we've just come along here. Over there,' he glanced up at a brick wall, 'is the canal and, beyond that, the railway line. The goods yards will be,' he turned to his right, 'behind those houses. Just to the north . . .'

Overhead, a few remaining dead leaves rustled in a light breeze. Jet could make out a bird settling its feathers somewhere in the lower branches. Far away, a clock chimed. Something stirred in her memory. She knew she had, once upon a time long ago, stood under another oak tree, with another man, on another night when all was dark and still.

Just after midnight, they returned to the headquarters. Hogan was given a mug of weak tea and Jet lapped at a basin of water.

'They're good folk round here,' Mr Spencer, the senior ARP warden, declared. 'Careful. I'll bet you didn't find a single light showing.'

'Not one,' Hogan agreed.

'And do you think you've familiarised yourself with the town?'

'I think so,' Hogan said. 'I was a bit lost by the canal but I've got it sorted out now.'

'Quite a maze of streets down there,' interrupted a police constable, who had just come in and was helping himself to the big, brown enamel tea pot simmering on a Valour oil stove. 'We call it the Casbah. Like in Arab cities. The place where all the thieves and ne'er-do-goods live. More burglars to the street down there than fleas on a dog's tail.' He smiled at Jet. 'Present company excepted, of course.' He sipped his tea and went on, 'And yet, do you know, since Jerry started his bombing, the crime rate's gone down by three quarters. Three-quarters!'

'Were you with the BEF in France?' Mr Spencer enquired.

'No. I got recalled six months ago,' Hogan replied.

'What were you in peacetime?'

'Electrician. My brother and I own a little shop. He's older than me, lost the sight of one eye in the Great War so he's out of this one. Now he's running the shop on his own.'

'You'd think the army would use your electrical skills,' the constable commented, refilling his mug. 'Trust them to get it wrong. My brother sails yachts. Races them. Went along to join up. Told them all he knew. So – guess what! – now he's in the RAF, mechanic, repairing Spitfires. I ask you!'

After a moment's silence, Mr Spencer patted Jet and said to Hogan, 'Do you think your dog'll be up to it? Once things hot up, it's no parade ground out there.'

'I'm sure she'll do very well,' Hogan responded.

'Well, let's hope so,' the constable said. 'God knows, we've needed you for the past few weeks. Civil defence are training their own dogs but, for the time being, there aren't enough to go round and the bigger cities get priority. We've only managed to get you because of the railway.'

'That's true,' Mr Spencer added. 'Jerry likes railways.'

As dawn was breaking, Hogan and Jet returned to Mrs Hartop's house. She had just got up and was standing in her parlour in a dressing gown, her hair wrapped in curlers rolled in squares of newspapers. They did not speak. Hogan led Jet upstairs, washed his face and hands in a basin of warm water Mrs Hartop brought up for him. Then, after checking Jet's pads for wear, for she was not used to walking long distances on hard roads and pavements, he lay down on the bed and immediately fell asleep.

Jet remained awake a little longer, listening to the sounds of the day beginning from the other side of the black-out curtain. Within fifteen minutes, she too was fast asleep on her blanket.

The clock on the town hall, which Jet had heard on her first night's patrol, chimed midnight. The street was still and silent. On one side, all the houses with odd numbers were in deep shadow, but all those opposite were illuminated by moonlight. Their red brick walls looked as if they had been faintly whitewashed. The pavements and the slate roofs shone, for there had been a light shower of rain earlier in the night and they were still damp.

'Might as well switch on a beacon,' Hogan said morosely as he and Jet walked along in the shadows. 'You mark my words, my girl, Jerry'll be over before we find our beds. That's a bomber's moon up there.'

As if to prove him right, a strange sound started up from the other end of the town. It was joined by another, then another. At first, it was a low humming drone but it soon swelled to a higher pitch, which rose and fell rhythmically.

'Air raid warning,' Hogan exclaimed. 'Those sirens send a chill down my spine.'

Jet shook her head to see if she could rid herself of the ululating whine, but to no avail. It was not that the noise hurt her ears, but it made her uncomfortable. It seemed to fill her brain, blotting out her ability to hear anything else.

The sky was suddenly pierced by three strong beams of light. They waved to and fro like vast beckoning fingers, dancing off the few clouds remaining after the rain, then getting lost in the depths of space. Jet watched them with fascination. One of the beams stopped swinging around the sky and stayed fixed on a point close to a cloud.

'There they are,' Hogan hissed. 'Luftwaffe Heinkels. One-elevens, I'm certain.'

In the centre of the beam were two aircraft flying at a high altitude. They reached the cloud and disappeared behind it. The beam zipped across the cloud and waited. The aircraft reappeared in its centre. As they moved across the sky, so the beam followed them. The other beams soon found their own aircraft.

'Come, Jess!' Hogan commanded. 'We've work to do.'

They hurried through the streets towards the civil defence HQ. As they arrived, the first bombs fell at the other end of town, close to the railway and the canal. Inside, Jet could hear the explosions, though they were muffled by distance, the walls of the office and the sandbags piled at the door.

Within a minute, the telephone bell jangled. Mr Spencer picked it up, uttered a few curt orders and hung up.

'Sleeman Street!' he shouted.

Hogan and Jet ran outside to the motorbike. Jet jumped into the side-car and they were off. The shaded headlight was hardly needed. The night was now lit not only by the moon but also by a warm glow in the sky which tinged the clouds with pink.

As they raced through the streets, Jet could see other vehicles heading in the same direction. Twice, Hogan pulled over to allow a fire engine to tear by, the fireman in the front seat frantically ringing the bell hanging beside the windscreen.

Ahead of them, an ARP warden stood at the end of a street, blowing a warning whistle and frenziedly waving his arms. Turning a corner, Hogan and Jet were presented with a terrible sight. Three houses in a terrace were on fire. Flames shot up from the roofs with showers of attendant sparks. Every window flickered. Two fire engines were stopped across the street. Their hoses snaked out from them, but the arching columns of water pouring into the blazing buildings seemed to make no difference to the fire. On either side, six or seven houses had collapsed into piles of rubble. Smoke and dust drifted away on the wind caused by the flames. Behind them, an explosion filled the sky with a dull orange cloud as another bomb fell on the railway goods yard.

Hogan skidded the motorbike to a standstill as the ARP warden ran over.

'You the chap with the casualty dog?' he yelled over the sound of a roof caving in and the ringing of an ambulance bell.

'That's us,' Hogan replied. 'Where do you want us?'

'You can start on Number 43. Over there. Family of five. No bomb shelter in the garden so they must have been indoors . . .'

The street was littered with broken bricks, splintered wood, shattered window glass, which Jet tried her best to avoid, and household furniture, all of it smashed beyond repair. Hogan ran towards the first of the ruined houses, Jet at his heels. She needed no command to keep up with him.

The pavement was buried in rubble. Where the kerb had been, two men were frantically scrabbling at the fallen masonry with their bare hands. Neither of them spoke, such was their attention to their work.

'Right!' Hogan shouted to them. 'Leave off for a minute.'

'Leave off?' one of the men shouted back. 'There's folk under this lot.'

'You can't do anything with your hands. Not yet,' Hogan told them. 'Let the dog go over the site. Save your energy for when you know where to dig.'

The men glanced at each other and stepped back.

'I reckon the stairs are somewhere about there,' one of them said, pointing to the centre of the mound of brick and wood which had been someone's home. 'They'll have been under the stairs, you know. Like it says in the pamphlets. In case of a raid go under a table or the stairs. They had a cupboard under the stairs . . .'

A policeman arrived with a powerful torch which he switched on, saying, 'No use hiding now. Jerry knows what's what.'

With the torch shining on the ruins, Hogan bent down to Jet's side.

'Seek, Jess. Seek!' he said to her, his mouth close to her ear. 'There's a good girl.'

Jet set off onto the ruin. She had to tread carefully, for many of the bricks were loose. Some were also hot. Here and there, shattered rafters poked up through the débris and there was a strong smell of brick dust and gas mixed with the more delicate smell of food.

After going some metres, Jet stopped. Another scent reached her nostrils. It was that of a person. She could distinctly pick out the tang of sweat: it was similar to that of Mrs Hartop, filled with fear. For a few moments, she moved her head from side to side, trying to pinpoint exactly where it was coming from. The air filled once more with the wail of the siren, but now it was a continuous, even hum.

'That's the all clear,' a voice said on the street behind Jet. 'Now we can get stuck in.'

'You think they stood a chance?'

'The house caved in like a sand-castle.'

Jet waited until the siren faded. The only sounds left were the voices on the street, the sound of the flames crackling and spitting in the burning buildings, the hiss of water and the thrumming of the fire engines' pumps.

When she started to tilt her head again, Hogan shouted out, 'Quiet, everyone! The dog's picking something up.'

All the men fell silent. The firemen switched off their pumps. Jet cocked her head again. The sweaty smell still hung about her feet. She poked her nose into a narrow crevice between two large chunks of wall. It was barely wide enough to take her snout. She sniffed. The smell was stronger. Then she heard it. It sounded like a kitten mewing or a field-mouse squeaking. Balancing with her paws on either side of the crack, she turned and glanced over her shoulder at Hogan.

'She's found something!' Hogan shouted.

Six men clambered over the ruins. Hogan reached Jet first and stroked her head.

'Good girl! Good girl!' he praised her.

'Where are they?' asked the policeman with the torch.

Jet pawed at the crack.

'Down here!' Hogan said.

The men started to shift the tumble of bricks, passing them back to the street. For fifteen minutes, they toiled and cursed, slipped and strained their backs. At last, one of the men reached into the ruin and pulled out a little girl of about eight. She was wearing her night-dress, the pattern of flowers printed upon it grimed and filthy. She blinked her eyes as the men passed her from one to the other down to the street, where a nurse in a red cape and white cap carried her towards a waiting ambulance. Over the next ten minutes, the remainder of the family were brought out of the wreck of their home, the last to appear being the husband of the house.

Jet and Hogan did not see the family rescued. They were already at work on the site of the next house, but without such success. All Jet could find was one old lady, dead under a collapsed wall with her knitting still in her hand.

It was long past dawn when the search for any other survivors was called off. Hogan and Jet returned to the motorbike which was covered in a coating of brick dust and motes of ash.

'You did well, Jess,' Hogan said as he lowered himself on to the saddle, Jet awkwardly getting into the side-car. 'I'm proud of you.'

She looked at him. From his tone of voice, she knew he was proud of her, was pleased with her performance, and yet there were tears running down his cheeks, carving little channels through the dirt.

For five months, Hogan and Jet worked in the town, during which time the Germans completely destroyed the railway goods yard, severely damaged the canal and blew up both the town's cinemas, and Mrs Hartop became, at least as she put it 'for the duration' of the war, a dog-lover.

By the end of their first month's lodging with her, Mrs Hartop insisted on personally giving Jet her evening meal, frequently slipped her bits of rabbit or mutton, bought a bag of Spillers dog biscuits for her as evening treats 'seeing you're such a good little dog' and, on one occasion, when Hogan was laid up in bed with 'flu, she actually took Jet for a walk around the streets, showing her off to neighbours and friends as 'the brave dog what boards with me'.

As the weeks passed, the Luftwaffe bomber squadrons turned their attention away from the town to concentrate on the bigger cities where there were factories which manufactured war supplies, where railway networks joined and where power stations and gas works were sited. It followed that it was, therefore, only a matter of time before Hogan and Jet would be re-posted.

The notice came after there had been no bombs dropped on the town for eighteen days. A young woman in an Auxiliary Transport Service uniform appeared on Mrs Hartop's step one Sunday morning. Her messenger's motorcycle stood at the kerb.

'Sergeant Kenneth Hogan live here?' she enquired.

'Yes, he does, my dear, and his wonderful dog with him what has stayed here with me and saved over fifty people. I think the dog should get a medal. And Sergeant Ken, too. They're both brave as gladiators.' She saw the ATS girl was growing impatient: she had a lot of messages to deliver that morning. 'I'll fetch him down, dear.'

When Hogan read it, the message was curt and to the point: he and Jet were to immediately report to a bigger city. Several petrol coupons were attached to the message to fuel his motorbike.

'It's not bad news,' Mrs Hartop said, with a certain jollity. 'Bad news comes with the Post Office telegraph girl.'

'I'm afraid it is, Mrs Hartop,' Hogan replied. 'Jess and I are re-deployed to – well, another city.'

There were tears in Mrs Hartop's eyes as Jet jumped

into the side-car half an hour later. She dabbed at them with her apron and put two paper bags in the compartment under the little windscreen.

'Just a little picnic,' she smiled benevolently. 'Sandwiches for you, sergeant, and a little snack for Jess here. I expect you've got a long journey and it's such a lovely summer's day.'

Then, to Hogan's amazement, Mrs Hartop bent over and gave Jet an enormous hug, pressing the dog's head into her rather large bosom. Jet was almost overpowered by the scent of lavender water. A fine mist of talcum powder crept up her nose, making her pucker her snout.

Half-way to their destination, Hogan pulled the Norton in beside a wood. The sun shone down on them from a clear blue sky. In the nearby fields, the wheat was green, nearly a metre high and waving in a warm breeze. When he switched off the engine, the only sounds they could hear were rustling leaves and lark-song.

'You'd never think there was a war on,' Hogan remarked, as he sat down and leaned against an elm tree. 'It all looks so peaceful.' He glanced up to the sky. 'You can hear larks but you can never spy the little beggars.'

Jet raised her head. She could see the lark high in the sky, hovering and singing. She could also smell a hare somewhere upwind in the wheat.

'Well, let's see what Mrs Hartop's got for us,' Hogan said and he opened the paper bags. 'She has done us proud! I've got Marmite and lettuce sandwiches – and an apple – and you've got . . .' From Jet's bag he took out a small enamel bowl sealed with greaseproof paper. Jet could tell from the smell before it was opened what it contained: rabbit stew.

When they had eaten, Hogan lay back in the sunlight and Jet wandered off into the trees. It was cool under the canopy of branches. She snuffled about, picking up the scent of a dog-fox and finding the remains of his last meal, a pigeon with the feather stumps chewed. By a tumble of stones overgrown with brambles, she came upon a stoat which immediately vanished. At the far end of the wood, a large hole under a beech tree stank of badgers.

'Come, Jess!' Hogan called. 'Time to be on our way. No rest for the wicked. Or the righteous, come to that. Not in wartime.'

They reached the city just after seven o'clock. Hogan reported for duty at the nearest barracks and was given the address of his billet, a bed and breakfast hotel near the city centre.

'Not a very merry kip, I'm afraid,' said the billeting officer. 'Before the war, it was little more than a doss-house for travelling salesmen and actors at the repertory theatre. Now – well, shall we say it's not improved. The only good thing is that it's near the CD HQ where you're based.'

The officer could not have been more truthful. The Landsdowne Hotel, as the house was grandiosely named, smelled of boiled cabbage and old socks. Hogan's room was on the ground floor facing the street across what had perhaps once been a pretty little garden. It was now an area of cracked paving stones, mottled with black oil stains, where cars had been parked.

The manager of the hotel was a surly man with a glass eye and sallow skin. His first words on seeing Hogan and Jet walk through the door were, 'If this were peacetime, you'd not bring *that* –' he pointed at Jet and sneered disdainfully – 'in here.'

'No happy Mrs Hartop here,' Hogan observed as he unpacked his kit bag, putting his clothes in a rickety chest of drawers beside his bed. 'Still, we're not on holiday. We've a job to do.'

Their first job came three nights later.

The air raid started at a quarter past ten. The sirens had begun wailing whilst there was still a vestige of daylight lining the horizon and outlining the rooftops and chimneys. Hogan and Jet patrolled a wide road full of shops and a busy pub. No sooner had the alarm commenced than the pub emptied, men running in all directions, some cycling frantically along the road to get back to their wives and children, their sweethearts or their parents. Behind one house, Jet watched as a family of seven – two parents, four children and a grandmother – entered their Anderson shelter, half buried against the rear wall of their garden. The children each carried a teddy bear or a doll, the father held three candles in brass candlesticks, the mother hugged the family cat to her breast whilst the grandmother was burdened with a Bible in one hand and a budgerigar in a bamboo cage in the other.

The bombs started falling twenty minutes later. Some were land mines, some high explosive and some incendiaries. The searchlights picked the aircraft out as the anti-aircraft gunners, their batteries situated in the city's main park, opened fire. Puffs of black smoke erupted in the searchlight beams.

Hogan and Jet took cover by huddling against a low brick wall surrounding the edge of a cemetery. No one ever hid against a high wall: that could crash down and crush one to death.

A bomber suddenly appeared in one of the fingers of light probing the sky. It was almost directly over their heads. As the light struck the aircraft, a stick of bombs fell from the aircraft's belly. Hogan saw them, tightened the chin strap on his helmet and hunched over Jet, pressing as much of her as he could under his body.

The six bombs fell just across the cemetery, in a line about two hundred metres long. The blast waves seemed to punch the air, which slammed against the low wall, ripping the branches out of a nearby sycamore tree and flinging them against the front of the houses opposite. The sound of crashing glass mingled with the *crump! crump!* of the explosions, the first blast knocking the breath out of both man and dog.

The raid was soon over. Hogan stood up, gulping in air. Jet panted and coughed. Across the cemetery, a column of garish orange flame a hundred metres high was dancing in the sky.

'Jerry's hit the gas works,' Hogan gasped. 'Come, Jess.'

Side by side, they ran through the cemetery, rushing past crosses and angels, oblong headstones and little vases of flowers, all touched by the glow of fire.

The street, when they reached it, was in utter chaos.

None of the houses was on fire but neither was a single one of them unscathed. Roofs had caved in, walls collapsed, windows imploded, doors had been wrenched off and iron garden gates distorted. A parked car lurched to one side, its tyres shredded.

Within minutes the fire brigade arrived, accompanied by the police and a civil defence unit. The senior officer rushed over to Hogan's side.

'Glad you're here. Quite a baptism of fire for your arrival,' he looked around with a grimace, 'in our fair city.'

'Where do you want us to start?' Hogan asked.

'That one looks pretty bad,' the officer replied, indicating the end house in a terrace of six, all of which were badly damaged. 'Looks like it took the full blast.'

An ARP warden ran over and said, 'We've cut off the gas main and the electricity. It's all safe now.'

Hogan and Jet went quickly to the house. The end wall had fallen in, smashing through the three floors and bringing down the roof. A thin wisp of smoke eked out of the wreckage. The second floor had somehow half managed to withstand the impact and now stuck out into the open air. It had been a bedroom, the bed still in place, with a picture hanging askew on the wall above it and a chair by the side.

'Looks like a life-size doll's house,' a man standing nearby remarked as a torch shone over the scene.

'How many people lived here?' Hogan enquired.

'Two adults and a boy of eight,' answered the man. 'We've checked the shelter in the garden. No one out there.'

'Seek, Jess,' Hogan said and, just as she had done so many times before, Jet stepped on to the rubble and began her search.

It was not easy. She could hear no sound coming from beneath her, for bombs were still falling somewhere else in the city and aircraft still thrummed high overhead. As soon as a searchlight locked on to a target, anti-aircraft guns spasmodically opened fire. Also, the fire at the gas works hissed loudly, the flames making a rushing sound like an enormous waterfall. Every so often there was a loud report as a main exploded. What was more, she could not smell anything distinctly either, for the air was thick with the stink of burning rubber, coal and gas.

For twenty minutes, Jet ranged across the ruined house, climbing up the slope of the fallen wall, edging under broken beams and trying hard all the while to locate at least something which might, no matter how tenuously, be a living human being.

The all clear siren sounded. The gunfire and bombing ceased. At the same time, the gas works fire died down. At Hogan's command, the firemen and rescue workers stopped what they were doing and fell silent.

It was all Jet needed. Ignoring the last noise of the fire, she concentrated on her hearing, her ears pricked forward and her head close to every nook and cranny in the débris. Within minutes, she located the sound for which she had been straining. It was not breathing or crying, not a groan of pain or a muffled plea for help. It was the *dump-dump-dump!* of a human heart beating.

'She's got one!' Hogan yelled as he recognised her signal to him.

The waiting men came forward and the inevitable passing of chipped bricks and bits of wood began. It was a hard struggle, for the wall had not fragmented when it fell but come down in huge chunks, each piece the size of a dining room table. It was an hour before the torch shone on the face of a little boy, grimed with dirt and tears.

'Don't you worry, lad!' Hogan said, kneeling by the hole at the base of which the face stared up, confused and afraid. 'We're all here and we'll soon have you dug out.'

The men renewed their efforts now the boy had been located. Jet, in the meantime, had located his parents near the back of the building. They were together in an area which had been their kitchen, their lives saved by the heavy cast-iron cooker. The floor above had collapsed on them but the cooker had taken the brunt of the weight, creating a little cave in front of the oven door. It was here the adults were found. The father's arm was badly shattered and his skull was fractured, leaving him semi-conscious; yet the mother had suffered only cuts and bruises. As the ambulance took her husband away, the woman pleaded to stay.

'My little boy's in there,' she sobbed. 'My David.'

'We've found your son,' a fireman said, 'and he's alive but we've got yet to dig him out.'

'Thank God!' the woman muttered, adding, 'Can I see him? Be with him?'

The nurse attending to her held her arm, saying, 'Best

you let the rescuers get on with their work. You don't want to get in the way now, do you, dear?'

For half an hour, the men dug into the building. The occupants of the other houses being all accounted for, there was no need for Jet to be further employed, so she sat next to the wrecked car and watched Hogan and the other men at work. Everything seemed to be going all right until, suddenly, one of the rescuers let out a shout and everyone scrambled off the building.

'What is it?' the boy's mother cried out. 'Why are you stopping?'

The ARP warden started to blow on his whistle. Everyone the length of the street stopped whatever they were doing.

'I'm sorry,' the civil defence officer told the boy's mother, 'but we've had a bit of a complication. Right next to your lad there's an unexploded bomb. It's not going to go off, but we can't actually get him out without moving it. And we dare not do that. Jerry booby-traps some of his bombs. What we have to do now is sit tight and wait for the bomb disposal fellows.'

The woman paled and half-fainted, the nurse taking her towards a chair someone had retrieved from one of the other houses and placed in the road.

'What about the boy?' Hogan enquired as the woman was led away.

'Nothing we can do. Just have to leave him there. He doesn't seem injured, just trapped. Not bleeding, not in any pain so far as we can tell.'

Hogan looked from the remains of the house to Jet.

'Give me your torch, constable,' he said to a policeman standing nearby. Then, turning, he murmured, 'Come, Jess!'

'Where do you think you're going?' the ARP warden shouted as Hogan stepped on to the first slope of loose bricks. 'You can't go up there.'

Yet Hogan ignored him and so did Jet.

The boy lay at the bottom of a hole about three metres wide at the top and two metres deep, the tapering sides consisting of rubble from which protruded the black iron fin of a large bomb. Very carefully, Hogan eased his head and shoulders into the hole with Jet creeping on her belly at his side. The torch lay to their left.

'Hello,' said Hogan, 'my name's Ken. What's yours?'

'David,' the boy said timorously.

'Can you move your arm, David?'

'Yes, I think so.'

'Reach up to me then, David.'

The boy raised his right arm. Hogan leaned forward until their fingers met.

'Let's hold hands for a bit, David,' he suggested; the boy's fingers tightened on his own.

'Are my mummy and daddy there?'

'Your dad's a little hurt and he's gone off to the hospital but your mum's just down in the street waiting for us to get you out. It'll be a little bit longer because we have to wait for a few soldiers to come and help us.' Hogan shifted himself to let Jet come nearer to the boy. 'Do you like dogs?'

'Yes,' the boy answered as Jet edged a little further into the hole.

'This is Jess. She's mine. In fact, she was the one who found you because she's trained to discover people buried like you are.'

The boy smiled weakly and looked up at Jet.

'Thank you, Jess,' he said.

'She's a very brave dog,' Hogan continued and, for over half an hour, he told Jet's story of fighting with the BEF and Dunkirk, as he imagined it, and the true tale of her work in the seaport.

Just as he reached the end of the tale, someone touched his boot and a voice said, 'All right, sergeant, we'll take over.'

Hogan craned his head. Above him stood an army captain.

'The soldiers I told you about are here, David,' Hogan explained, 'so I'm going to leave you and they're going to carry on rescuing you.'

As he let go of Hogan's hand, the boy asked, 'Can Jess stay?'

Hogan glanced at the captain who made no reply but shook his head.

'The dog's not going to get in the way,' Hogan whispered. 'She'll not hamper you. Superb training. Been an IPD before this. Taken off the beaches at Dunkirk . . .'

The captain thought for a moment then went on, 'Very well. She might serve a good purpose, keep the little chap calm. Might keep us calm too, eh, corporal?'

A corporal with a grim look on his face and carrying a heavy satchel nodded his agreement.

'Stay, Jess,' Hogan instructed her quietly.

Jet looked at her master. She did not understand what

was going on but she sensed things were serious. Hogan retreated to the street and Jet edged further into the hole until her head was close to the boy's. She pushed her left paw out towards him and he took hold of it as if it was Hogan's hand: then, nuzzling the boy's brow, she gave him one wet lick.

The captain smiled and said, 'Right, corporal, let's take a look at Adolf Hitler's parcel.'

It was a slow process. The two bomb disposal men had to shift more bricks from the bomb casing. Then, locating a steel plate in the side, they slowly unscrewed it to reveal a series of wires and connectors. All the time they worked, Jet stayed close to the boy, her breath tickling his forehead, her paw warm and hard in his fingers. The plate removed, the two soldiers studied the layout of the interior of the bomb and withdrew to the street to compare the circuitry to plans they had in a leather-covered wallet. At length, they folded away their diagrams of German bombs.

'So what do you think, corporal?' the captain asked.

'Don't know, sir. It's like the one we had last week in Coventry, but it's different. That green wire was red in Coventry. And there's a trembler. If we touch that before we disconnect it, it'll be Guy Fawkes Night and you and I will have wings and be singing hymns.'

'What's the problem, sir?' Hogan asked.

'The bomb's not standard, sergeant,' the captain explained. 'We keep a record of every one we attend to. That way, when we meet another, we know immediately how to deal with it. This is a standard 1000 pound bomb but it's been wired . . . To be blunt, we're a bit nonplussed.'

'Nothing for it, sir,' the corporal said, 'but to cut the blue wire and pray like hell.'

'I have to agree with you, corporal,' the captain replied and, turning to the ARP warden said, 'Clear the street.'

Everyone was guided to the end of the street two hundred metres away. Hogan remained with the bomb disposal team.

'I think you'd better go as well, sergeant,' the captain suggested.

'My dog's up there,' Hogan said quietly. 'I'm not leaving her.'

The men exchanged glances. They were soldiers. They knew how important loyalty and friendship were in time of war.

'Very well,' the captain agreed. 'Let's get on with it.'

They reached the hole. The little boy was still holding Jet's paw.

'What's happening?' he asked in a weak voice.

'We're just going to see to this,' the captain answered, 'then we'll get you out.'

Hogan held the torch. The captain steadied a pair of insulated pliers, holding the blue wire away from the others. Then, putting a stethoscope to his ear, he pressed the end to the casing of the bomb. The corporal positioned his wire-cutters.

'Here goes,' he muttered.

Jet could sense the men's nerves. They were taut, filled with fear. Their sweat smelled of it.

The corporal squeezed his hand and the wire-cutters clicked. As soon as the wire was cut, he looked at the captain. Five seconds ticked by like minutes. Then the officer shook his head.

'Nothing,' he said, his voice seeming loud after the tension. 'Not a tick. Not a whirr. You've pulled it off, corporal. Well done!'

The three men sighed with relief. Jet, sensing the tension was over, wagged her tail.

'Sergeant,' the captain said, 'call them all back. It's disarmed.'

In another twenty minutes, to the cheering of the people watching, the little boy was pulled out of the wreckage. His pyjamas were torn and his leg was badly bruised but he was otherwise unscathed. When he reached the street, his mother rushed forwards and hugged him tightly as she carried him to the ambulance. As he was about to get into the vehicle, the little boy turned.

'Where's Jess?' he asked.

Hogan called her over.

'Good-bye, Jess,' the little boy said and, stretching from his mother's arms, touched her on the tip of her wet, cold snout.

AUTUMN 1942

'Atten-*SHUN*!'

The regimental sergeant-major's voice echoed over the parade ground. Several thousand pairs of heavy, black army boots slammed down on the concrete.

'By the right, quick *MARCH*!'

The band struck up and the soldiers set off out of the barracks and through the town. Each soldier wore his battle-dress, his rifle sloped over his left shoulder, his right arm swinging in time with his step and the beat of the drum. At the head of the procession, the King's and regimental colours were carried fluttering from staffs, the list of battle honours embroidered around the regimental crest.

Every street down which the soldiers passed was lined with cheering women and running children. Shopkeepers stood in their doorways to wave. Policemen and ARP wardens saluted. By the town clock, a young woman ran out of the crowd and pinned a red rose on to Fred's tunic. For the rest of their march, the heady perfume of the flower drifted up to him, mixed with the smell of gun oil from his rifle and blanco from the webbing straps of his infantryman's 37 pattern equipment.

At the docks, the troops formed lines as they waited to climb the gangway on to the troopship. Towards the bows, cranes were lifting military vehicles and crates of equipment up to the decks.

'Looks big, doesn't it?' said a private standing by Fred. 'The ship, I mean.'

'Yes,' Fred replied, the soldier's words bringing his thoughts back from Crayham Woods: the hooting of a ship's horn had reminded him of tawny owls and moonlit nights.

'I'm really glad we're posted to North Africa. You know what I'm looking forward to?' the private went on. 'I'm looking forward to riding a camel. I've seen them at the zoo, but I've never seen one in the desert.'

'I don't suppose any of us have,' Fred responded, pausing for a moment before adding, 'and I don't suppose any of us will have much chance. We're going to fight Rommel's Panzer tanks, not go camel racing.'

'And I'd like to see the pyramids of Egypt,' the private carried on, undeterred. 'And the Sphinx.'

'You know what they call him in our platoon?' another private addressed Fred. 'They call him Traveller. He says the war's his way to see the world cheap. You know what he's got in his pack? An atlas!'

The line shuffled forward and Fred reached the foot of the gangway. He had not taken three steps up it when he was sure he heard a dog bark. It was ridiculous: he knew that the moment he turned round. There was no chance whatsoever the dog on the dock behind him was Jet. Yet, despite himself, even after so long he stopped and looked. Below him were rows and rows of soldiers. Not a dog, indeed no animal at all, was to be seen.

'You! Move on!' a harsh voice called out.

Fred went on up the gangway and entered the ship, where he was directed to a cabin with four bunks in it. The other three were already occupied by two privates and a lance corporal.

'Not bad!' the latter commented. 'It must have been a passenger ship in peacetime. We've got our own private loo.'

Swinging his kit on to his bunk, Fred went up several flights of stairs to the boat deck. The side rail of the vessel was jammed with soldiers all looking out at the town across the roofs of the dockside warehouses, taking their last look at England.

'I wonder how many of us won't see home again,' pondered a thin-faced young man leaning against one of the lifeboats.

'Don't talk like that!' said an older man with a red scar on his cheek. 'Keep your chin up. You'll be back.'

Fred did not bother to look at the town. He was too busy scanning the quay to see if, by some strange but wonderful quirk of fate, Jet was posted to the same troopship. Yet there was no dog to be seen below.

'You didn't see a dog come aboard, did you?' he asked the man with the scar.

'A dog?' he replied. 'Our regimental mascot's a goat. And he isn't coming on this little cruise.'

'No, you don't understand,' Fred said urgently. 'Not a mascot. A military dog. A messenger dog or a casualty dog, a patrol dog – that sort of thing.'

'I don't think we're taking dogs,' the soldier rejoined. 'Not a lot of use in the desert. And they wouldn't like it. No trees for them to swing their legs against!' He roared with laughter at his joke.

Going below decks once more, Fred found his cabin. The other three occupants were out. He lay on his back on his bunk, his feet towards the porthole. His heart was heavy and there was a choking lump in his throat. As the ship slipped her mooring ropes and edged away from the dock, he thought if only he could have seen Jet just once more before he went off to fight the Germans, given her just one more stroke for luck. For love.

Never mind, he consoled himself, as the ship began to shudder under the turn of her propellers. Once the Germans were defeated in North Africa he would be back in England and then he could return to his quest to find Jet.

Little did he know that, after the baking deserts of Egypt and Libya, he was to visit other foreign countries before landing on the coast of England once again.

'I don't need to tell you,' Hogan said as he sat in the garden under the apple tree, Jet curled in the shade by the side of his chair, 'the tide of this war is changing. The Germans are starting to have a hard time of it and that's the truth. It's not just a matter of morale-boosting on the BBC. It's a fact.'

Phillie saw her father's tea cup was empty and, reaching for the pot on the garden table, refilled it for him. Cassie offered him another slice of bread and margarine with a thin smearing of not-very-sweet, wartime jam, but Hogan politely refused it.

'As I was saying,' he continued, 'the war's moving our way. The RAF is regularly bombing Germany and we've driven Jerry right out of North Africa. Admittedly, we are getting a bit of a hammering from the Japanese in Burma but the Americans are starting to snap at their heels. The Russians are stopping the German advance.'

He sipped at his tea. A crow landed on the fence and started to caw.

'That blessed bird!' Mrs Hogan complained. 'He's been after the apples for days now. Jess! See Goering off!'

Jet got up to obey but the crow was already in flight, alarmed by Hogan's roar of laughter.

'Goering!' he cried. 'Whose idea was it to call him after Hitler's *Reichsmarschall*?'

Yet his humour soon faded, for Hogan had something serious to tell his family.

'There's going to be a new offensive,' he said, stroking Jet's head as she settled down once more. 'Naturally, I can't tell you anything about it. It's all secret. Indeed, I don't know where it is and I'm not going to repeat the rumours I hear in the sergeant's mess. Rumours can be as dangerous and as harmful as the truth in wartime. All I do know is . . . Well, I'm being recalled to active service.'

There was a stunned silence. Mrs Hogan put her hand to her mouth. The girls looked at their father. Jet glanced up, sensing the emotion passing between them.

At length, Cassie broke the silence, saying, 'Will you be gone for long, Daddy?'

'There's no way of knowing,' her father replied. 'All I am told is I'm to be posted.'

'When?' Mrs Hogan asked, her voice quiet with apprehension.

'Next week. This will be my last leave for a while. What I can tell you is I'm being sent to an infantry division. I'll still be working with dogs and . . .'

He did not need to say it. The family knew what was coming next.

'You'll be taking Jess,' Mrs Hogan said.

'Yes. I don't think she's so lame that she couldn't be of tremendous use. I know she hasn't been working – not properly working – for over nine months now, what with the bombing lessening, but she won't have forgotten a single trick. Of that I'm quite certain. And I can't think of any other animal I would rather go into battle with.'

'You will look after her, won't you, Daddy?' Phillie asked, tears in her eyes.

'You know I will and, what's more, I know she'll look after me. We'll be back, don't you worry.'

Three days later, Jet and Hogan were sitting together in the guard's van of a train heading south through the English countryside. The van door was open, a warm wind blowing in on them, occasionally laden with smuts of soot from the locomotive. Beyond the hedgerows and trackside telegraph poles, a landscape of fields and villages, small towns and church steeples, rivers and bridges and roads and lanes slid by, all bathed in a balmy summer sunshine.

The sky had been overcast for most of their voyage. A fierce storm had lashed them for hours, the wind only dropping as they came closer to their destination, the sea lessening but still running with a metre-high swell. A weak sun began to shine down on the soldiers in the landing craft, slightly lifting their spirits.

Hogan checked his Sten gun. Despite the salt spray cascading over the square bow ramp, it was in good working order. He had given it an extra thick coating of oil the night before. Jet sat on her haunches beside him, her body swaying to the motion of the clumsy vessel as it hit the waves, rolling and pitching awkwardly. All around her, men prepared in their own private ways for battle. Some sat quietly in thought, some had a far-away look in their eyes, some checked and re-checked their weapons as Hogan had done; several muttered silent prayers and a few stood facing the distant shoreline of Sicily. Quite a number of them looked pale with seasickness: the bilges stank of acrid vomit at which Jet puckered up her nose.

'So that's Italy,' commented the colour sergeant standing beside Hogan. 'I somehow thought it was going to be sunny. You know, a land of wine and grapes and pretty girls and suchlike.'

'It'll be hot enough for you in an hour,' the sergeant major interrupted. 'When we hit that beach you'll think the flames of hell are like the candles on your birthday cake.'

Yet he was wrong. The landing craft ran up on the beach without so much as a single shot being fired at it. The Italian army thought no one would invade through a storm at sea, and the German garrison of the island had been tricked by British espionage into believing they were going to invade Sardinia instead.

Hogan led his platoon inland from the beach, heading for an Italian command post half a mile from the coast across a vineyard. Edging along the rows of vines, the grapes hanging from the branches, they approached the building cautiously. The walls had been painted in camouflage stripes. Beside the main door, a Fiat staff car was parked under a tree.

'See anything?' Hogan whispered to his corporal.

'Nothing.'

Yet Jet knew what lay ahead. It was not a mine or a trip-wire, not a hidden ambush of Italian soldiers. It was a large, nondescript dog lying somewhere close to the parked car. She looked into Hogan's face which was level with her own, for the platoon were crouching for their final assault. He caught her eye and, in that moment, something told him to let her go ahead.

'Seek, Jess,' he whispered and he unclipped her leash.

Jet set off towards the building. When she reached the corner, she stopped and made a little whine. The large dog sat up and glanced round: then he saw Jet and rose to his feet. He was tethered by a long chain to the tree. Jet wagged her tail and walked slowly towards the dog. It did not growl, but also wagged its tail.

'Look at that!' the corporal hissed. 'If we'd gone on, that big brute would have barked his head off.'

The platoon moved forwards. By the time they reached the parked car, their weapons cocked and ready, Jet and the dog were sniffing at each other.

'Nose to bum,' the corporal murmured. 'The universal dog's hello.'

Hogan signalled to his men. They fanned out, covering the surroundings and the approach track from a road several hundred metres away. Hogan and two others quietly opened the door and entered the post, their Sten guns ready. The communications room was empty. The radio equipment was switched on, but the volume knob was switched to zero. Next door were the sleeping quarters from which Hogan could clearly hear the sound of snoring. He entered and stared at the sight before him. Ten Italian soldiers were fast asleep on bunks. They were not even dressed but lay in their underwear.

'*Buon giorno!*' Hogan announced loudly, using the only Italian phrase he knew. 'Time to get up.'

The Italian soldiers stirred in their bunks, opened their eyes, took one look at Hogan's Sten gun and, swinging their legs to the floor, slowly put their hands over their heads.

'Piece of cake!' declared the corporal as the Italians lined up outside. 'And all because our pooch did a bit of flirting.'

By midday, the beach landings were consolidated, camps were set up and defensive trenches dug, with patrols moving inland searching out enemy units. They met with little resistance, almost every road block, pillbox and sentry post being either abandoned before they arrived or manned by Italian troops who instantly welcomed the invaders by surrendering their weapons.

As evening closed in, Hogan's platoon joined up with two others to take a small village on the side of a hill. They expected to come under fire. The village was in a commanding position and just one well-placed machine gun could have played havoc with their advance. Yet nothing happened. They reached the outskirts of the houses without firing a shot and, within ten minutes, had secured the whole place. The soldiers moved from house to house, swinging open doors and levelling their guns; all they found were families huddling anxiously in their homes. When they realised the British soldiers meant them no harm, they tentatively waved at them. Some even presented them with bottles of wine and lumps of hard, salty cheese.

Once they were sure the village posed no threat, sentries were posted around the perimeter, the soldiers digging themselves into an olive grove to the west of the church.

'I thought we were fighting a war,' the corporal said. 'This is more like Cowboys and Indians in a school playground.'

'These are Italian troops,' Hogan pointed out as they settled themselves around a solid fuel hexamine stove on which a mess tin of tea was brewing. 'They don't want to fight. They want peace, want to go back to their families and their countryside, get on with their own lives.'

'So do we, sergeant,' muttered a voice from beside the roots of a gnarled olive tree.

'Mark my words,' Hogan warned, 'it'll be different when we meet Jerry.'

Once it grew dark, Hogan walked Jet through the olive grove until they came to a low stone wall. Hogan sat down, Jet next to him. The sky was a mass of stars. Far down the hillside, an owl hooted mournfully. In the distance, a small farm nestled between trees, its sun-bleached pantiled roof washed faintly white by the starlight.

'What are we doing here, Jess?' he pondered aloud. 'We should be at home with our loved ones, not wandering about some foreign land.' A meteor briefly burned against the satin darkness of space. 'Wouldn't it be good,' he carried on, 'if men were like dogs? Like you were today. Straight off the beach and palling up with a duffer of an

Italian mutt. Same language, same idea.' He grinned to himself and patted her head, ruffling her ears. 'Mind you, you had an ulterior motive. I'm sure of that.'

They returned to where the men were bivouacked.

'You know what I fancy?' one of the soldiers mused as he sipped his tea. 'I fancy a roast beef sandwich. With a bit of horseradish.'

'Or mustard,' said someone else.

'I'd like a leg of roast chicken,' the corporal declared. 'Not fussy about the vegetables. Or the gravy. Or the bread sauce. Just the bird would do me nicely.'

'We couldn't cook it,' said the roast beef lover, adding, 'not over our little stoves.'

'Yes, we could,' the corporal answered. 'Just over there, there's a depression surrounded by a few low walls, all crumbling down. Looks like there was a hut there once. We could light a fire in that. Plenty of dead olive branches lying about. No one would see it except from an aircraft. And I don't hear any Jerry recce flights going over. Besides, the trees would give cover. And as for the smoke, anyone would think it was a shepherd or coming from a house or . . .' He stopped himself. 'I think I'll dream of something else,' he said. 'My mouth's watering.'

Hogan listened to the men's conversation then, tapping the corporal on the shoulder, said, 'Take over for a few minutes.'

With Jet at his side, Hogan made his way back to the stone wall. Slipping over the stones, they headed downhill, following a narrow footpath which wended its way from the valley floor up to the village. Wherever the path dropped over the edge of a terrace, Hogan stopped and surveyed the shadows. He was sure there were no enemy troops in the vicinity: but then, it was not Germans he was concerned about.

After ten minutes walking, they reached the outskirts of the farm. It was a meagre place. The farmhouse was a low, single storied building with a cobbled yard in which was parked a horse-drawn trap and an ancient wooden plough. Across the yard was a stable, the door of which was open. From within came the shuffle of a horse standing on straw.

The various odours of the farmyard mingled into a confusing mixture. Jet, pausing with Hogan in the shadows of a cypress tree about twenty metres from the edge of the cobbles, delicately sniffed the air. Apart from horse and the musty aroma of hay, she picked up the scents of human along with those of goat, chicken, cow, cat, rat and mouse, pigeon and dog.

The farm was still: the farmer and his family, aware there were invading soldiers in the vicinity, were keeping their heads down.

For some minutes, Hogan studied the layout of the farm. Behind the stable was a small paddock, at the far end of which was a low stone building; it was, he reasoned, a pig-sty. Very cautiously, keeping to the shadows, he and Jet moved to their right. As they shifted position, more of the farm came into view. Tethered to a post was a dark-coloured cow. It was sitting down, its front legs tucked under its bulky frame, glumly chewing the cud. Moving further to the right, a small vegetable plot became visible, with several rows of tomato plants and a watermelon vine growing along the ground. The melons were bigger than footballs. Across the vegetable plot was what Hogan had been searching for – a small wooden shed with a sloping, flat roof raised off the ground on six large stones.

Signalling to Jet to stay at heel, he crouched down and headed for this little building. It was a ramshackle affair. A window in one side was filled with a lattice of interwoven sticks. The door, hung on hinges made of strips of leather and held closed by a wooden latch, was approached by a plank leaning against the sill.

Hogan watched the farm for signs of movement. Nothing seemed to stir except the sideways slide of the cow's lower jaw. He strained his ears. Only the grinding of the cow's teeth and the shuffle of the horse's hooves could be heard.

Reaching up, Hogan raised the wooden latch on the shed door and signalled to Jet to enter. As she put her forepaws on the plank, he whispered, 'Seek.'

Jet entered the shed. All around the walls were nailed boxes whilst, above her, several tree branches had been wedged across the interior. The boxes and the branches were lined with sleeping chickens. The floor was a soft carpet of dried chicken droppings and discarded feathers.

For a moment, Jet stood in the centre of the hen-house. Something in her memory stirred. She had done this before. Not with chickens, but with pheasants being raised for the autumn sportsmen's guns.

The trick was not to alarm the birds. If she moved slowly she could lift them off their perches, one by one, with hardly a flutter of wings.

She edged towards the rear and, with infinite patience, raised her head and closed her jaws on a plump hen sitting on a nest box. It shook its feathers as her mouth closed on it but it did not struggle. As she lifted it clear of the wood, the hen next to it shifted over to occupy its space.

As her head appeared around the hen-house door, Hogan reached up, took the chicken from her jaws and promptly wrung its neck.

Jet returned to the perches and surreptitiously caught two more hens. Like the first, they put up no struggle in the darkness and she delivered them to Hogan with not so much as a mark upon them. Her soft, gun-dog's mouth instinctively avoided breaking the skin of her prey. When Hogan received them, the only sign they had been in a dog's mouth was the thin slaver of canine spittle on their feathers.

'Seek, Jess,' Hogan whispered again as he despatched the third chicken. 'Just one more.'

It was their undoing. Jet took a firm hold on the hen but, as Hogan put his fingers round it, it fluttered free and flew off in the direction of the cow. Landing by the beast, it startled it. The cow rose unsteadily to its feet. This, in turn, alarmed the chicken. It squawked, just once. Yet this was enough. From the rear of the stable appeared a huge mongrel dog, its chain rattling as it moved. No sooner had it caught sight of Jet, then Hogan, than it started barking hysterically.

Hogan snatched up the three dead hens and started off across the paddock at a crouching sprint. Jet kept to his heels. As they reached the wall of the paddock, the farm door opened, the faint gleam of an oil lamp cutting a square across the cobbles.

'*Chi questo?*' an angry voice called out.

Hogan made no reply. He and Jet ran to the footpath and headed off up the hill, the chickens hanging from his hand.

As they approached the olive grove, a sentry challenged them.

'Advance and be recognised,' he hissed.

'Hogan.'

The sentry beckoned them forward. Hogan and Jet went quickly through the olive grove to where the corporal and five or six others were lying or sitting on the ground.

'Corporal,' Hogan ordered as he tossed the chickens at the corporal's feet, 'get a detail up to gather some firewood. And you,' he nodded in the direction of a lance corporal, 'clear that depression.'

Within a quarter of an hour, the soldiers had a fire burning in the secrecy of the depression, the glimmer of the flames dancing off the remains of the stone walls. A thin drift of grey smoke rose through the branches of the overhanging olives. The chickens, plucked, drawn and gutted, were skewered and sizzling on wooden spits. The aroma of roasting chicken drifted through the trees.

When the hens were cooked, the soldiers queued up to collect their share of what Hogan informed them were spoils of war. The sentries were taken their portions. For ten minutes, everyone was silent save for the sounds of forks against mess tins and the sucking clean of fingers.

Hogan presented Jet with two slices of breast and the meat from a wing.

When the birds were little more than skeletons, Hogan dropped the remains of the carcasses into the fire where the bones crackled and snapped. It was an important precaution, to prevent Jet scavenging any of them during the night. He knew, as every handler did, the bones of fowl could splinter in a dog's belly and, causing internal bleeding, kill it.

'Wonderful!' the corporal said, lying back on his groundsheet with a contented grin on his lips. 'A stroke of genius that was, sir. Did you have any bother? We heard a dog barking way off down the valley.'

'It was all my fault,' Hogan admitted. 'Jess here was marvellous. She went into that hen-house like a true professional. You'd think she'd been doing it all her life. Took the birds off their roosts without so much as a bent feather. All was going well until I was too slow in wringing one of the blighter's necks. It took off, the dog woke up and the farmer turned out.' He stroked Jet's back. 'I'll tell you something, corporal. When this war's over, if I can't get my old job back, I could certainly team up with Jess here and turn my hand to poaching.'

Those not on watch turned in, lying huddled in shallow depressions scooped in the earth. Hogan settled himself onto his groundsheet, Jet curling up on the bare earth between the roots of an olive tree, close to his head. As he fell asleep, Hogan could feel Jet's warm, moist breath on his face. It smelt of roast chicken.

*

From behind the rock, Hogan surveyed the lie of the land ahead of them in the dawn light. For about two hundred metres, it rose gently through an orchard of lemon trees, the fruit just beginning to turn from green to yellow. Beyond the orchard was a stone terrace wall, behind which there lay, according to the map he held, a flat field of sun-scorched grass: then, a little higher up, there was a dirt track and a bank four metres high leading to the wall of the monastery of San Martino.

It was not a large monastery. It consisted of four buildings, a stable and a church with a *campanile*, a tall tower containing a single bell, surrounded by a three-metre wall. Under normal circumstances, the soldiers would have ignored it but for one fact: it had a commanding view of the valley beyond.

'Do you think they're still there?' the corporal enquired in a whisper.

'Jerry?' Hogan answered. 'I should think so.' He glanced at his watch. 'Ten minutes to go. Remember, we hold back. We're in reserve. Our job's to locate casualties and get them back.'

'I'm glad we're in support on this one,' the corporal said. 'It was all right being on the attack when we landed. Everyone had to play their bit. Besides, all the Italians were still having a kip. But now! I'm just glad we're not primarily fighters but savers.'

Jet sat patiently behind another rock. At some stage in the not-too-distant past, the monks must have kept goats near the rocks. She could smell them everywhere. Small pellets of goat droppings littered the earth, reminding her of rabbit dung. What was worse, she kept getting bitten by ticks, attracted to the area by the goats. Every few minutes, she had to have a scratch where one was making its way through her fur. Hogan helped. Every hour, he checked her over. When he found a tick sucking at her skin, he did not pull it off. That could be dangerous, for although he might remove its body, he could leave the parasite's head fixed to Jet, which would turn the bite septic and sore. Instead, he borrowed a cigarette from one of the privates and burned the tick off: as soon as the hot ember touched it, it would let go and drop to the ground. Hogan would then squash it with his boot, leaving a stain of Jet's blood in the dusty earth.

'Five minutes,' Hogan hissed. The platoon members exchanged glances. Several fingered their weapons.

Up ahead, in the grey dawn light beneath the lemon trees, Hogan could see vague shapes on the ground. They might have been rocks sticking out of the soil but he knew otherwise. They were soldiers, British soldiers, ready to move against the monastery. Above them, the monastery wall looked foreboding.

'Three minutes,' Hogan murmured.

At exactly twenty minutes to seven, the first soldiers rose from the ground and advanced towards the monastery. Hogan studied the top of the wall through a pair of field binoculars. Nothing moved.

We're going to pull it off, he thought. Jerry's left the monastery. It's going to be a walk-over.

Through the binoculars, he saw a small black object arcing through the air. At first, he thought it was a bird, a falcon perhaps, diving on its prey. He followed it through the air, watching as its trajectory dropped. It disappeared into the citrus trees. There was an explosion. The ground erupted in an inverted cone of soil and stones from which smoke billowed out. It was another two seconds before the sound hit him, followed by the dull blast wave. Another of the birds came winging over.

'Grenades!' he yelled. 'Take cover!'

Jet, sitting behind her rock, did not flinch. When the blast wave arrived, she prickled her hackles but otherwise she showed no sign of noticing the start of the offensive.

Up ahead, the soldiers in the lemon grove were returning fire, their Sten guns rattling a fierce tattoo of reports. Bullets spat off the monastery walls. Pieces of plaster dusted from the outside of the *campanile*. The air began to mist with gun smoke and the tart stench of cordite drifted through the trees.

From not far behind Jet there started a dull, intermittent thudding noise, like someone bouncing a half-inflated football on a stone floor. It was a sound she had not heard before. Turning, she saw three small groups of soldiers dropping small metal cylinders into an upright tube. A moment later, the tube puffed out smoke and the noise occurred.

Hogan, noticing Jet had seen this, explained, 'Mortars. They're lobbing mortars at Jerry,' just as if she was a raw recruit who needed to be kept informed of what was going on.

By now, the front line of men had advanced at least seventy metres towards the monastery. It was time for Hogan's platoon to follow. Signalling them by hand – his voice could not be heard over the sounds of battle – he left the cover of the rocks and started to crawl towards the lemon trees. He did not need to give an order to Jet. She followed him, crouching down until her belly rubbed the floor.

As they advanced, several of the men fired short bursts from their guns. It was not that they had a target in mind other than the bulk of the monastery. It was more a need to fire in order to feel they were defending themselves.

Some way into the trees was a pile of stones collected from the ground: perhaps the trees' owner had intended to build something. Hogan, the corporal and Jet gained the protection of the stones without mishap. Every minute or so, a bullet whined off the pile but nothing could penetrate it.

Cautiously, Hogan peered round the stones. Up ahead, the British were still under fire. Being closer to the monastery now, Hogan could see a German machine-gun nest near the corner of the building, with another positioned behind a thin, medieval window close to the base of the wall.

'They'll need to knock those out,' the corporal observed. 'Once our lads get to the track, they'll be pinned down in the crossfire.'

Over the din of the small-arms fire, the thumping of the mortar and its muffled explosions, there came a distant rumble, like summer thunder in far-off hills.

'Get down!' Hogan yelled at the top of his voice.

Less than a second later, a powerful explosion shook the ground and punched the air. The trees swayed and cracked. Heavy boughs were tossed across the sky. Half-ripe lemons fell to bounce on the rocks. A confetti of leaves showered down.

Hogan had his binoculars to his face. Far down in the valley, not far from a small hamlet of houses, he saw three puffs of dense, blue-grey smoke. They could only mean one thing: German artillery had sneaked in behind them.

Three more explosions tore through the trees, a hundred metres to the left. They were mingled with screams.

'You must have really got on that farmer's wick!' the corporal hollered. 'He's called up his pals. All you did was nick a few scrawny hens. Just as well you didn't listen to the roast beef eaters and pinch the cow.'

He pitched forward, his left hand out in front of him, his right trying to reach over his back as if he had an itch in the place no one can reach. By the time he hit the dusty ground, he was dead.

For a moment, Jet did not move: then her training took over. She sniffed at the corporal, her nose brushing his ear. Just as she had known when the chickens were dead in Hogan's fist, or the pheasants dead in the sack in those long-lost days around Crayham, she knew with a canine instinct hidden deep within her mind that he was not alive.

The British soldiers were trapped. Guns in the monastery kept them with their heads down, whilst the artillery in the valley bombarded them. The air was quickly filled with a choking fog of dust, leaves and bitter-smelling smoke. They were taking casualties.

After twenty minutes, there was a lull in the fighting

which offered a chance for Hogan and his men to gather as many of the injured as they could; even if the battle was not over, it was essential to treat as many soldiers as possible to prevent gangrene setting into their wounds. The pile of stones afforded good cover for first-aid treatment. Hogan looked at Jet and, briefly touching her head for encouragement, said, 'Good girl, Jess. Seek!'

She needed no other instruction. With a trusting obedience, she ran out from behind the pile of stones and headed up the hill. She had not gone fifty metres when the fighting flared again. Bullets spattered into the ground around her. A grenade, exploding in a tree close to her, sprayed her with pieces of wood: fortunately, they were not sharp and no splinters stuck in her flesh.

Beneath a felled lemon tree, she found her first soldier. He was pinned by the waist under a heavy bough. His hands were twitching but he was dead. She moved on. Nearby, a second dead soldier lay on the ground. He was a young man with curly brown hair and a freckled face. There was a vague smile on his lips but he was past laughter now.

She ran on. One of the German machine-gunners got her in his sights and fired a long burst. The bullets struck the ground behind her then cut a line through the trunk of a tree but nothing hit her.

One of the artillery shells hit within thirty metres. The explosion picked Jet up, hurled her through the air then dropped her like a rag doll beside a scrubby bush. She was winded, gasped for air, her mouth gulping it in regardless of the grit and grime. For several minutes, she lay on her side, panting hard, trying to get her lungs to work properly again. When, at last, she felt she could go on, she stood up and went behind the bush.

Somewhere nearby, she heard a man groaning. It was a deep, recurrent noise.

Jet approached the man with her belly to the dirt. He was lying with the top half of his body in a shallow, dry ditch, his legs on the bank. His trousers were black with blood-soaked soil. Slipping down into the ditch, Jet edged towards the man's head. He had lost his helmet and had a deep gash just above his right ear.

He was muttering, his words making no sense.

'Watch the pixies!' he gabbled. 'Look at the little pixies' hats!'

He opened his eyes. Jet's face was less than a metre from his own. He squinted, trying to focus through the pain. His hand crept up to his face, smearing the blood oozing from his scalp.

'What are you doing here?' he whispered hoarsely, his lips hardly moving, but the words coming out. 'Get out of it!'

He tried to shoo Jet away, his hand leaving his face and making vague circles in her direction.

Jet lay quite still. Just over her head, small zips cut the air. They might have been high speed wasps, yet she knew they were not: they were the unseen high-pitched whistling things which caused pain, one of those which had hit her when she and Turpin were queuing in the sea.

The wounded man stared at the dog for a moment, reaching out with his blood-caked fingers until they touched her black fur.

'Jet,' he said softly, like a man talking in his sleep. 'You'd best get home, Jet.'

For a moment, Jet studied the man. He was unshaven. His clothing stank of cordite and blanco and Brasso polish and sweat.

Sweat. Jet pushed her nose against the man's arm. His sleeve was torn to the elbow and hung in tatters like a scarecrow's coat. His skin was crusted with dirt. Yet there was something familiar about him, something she half recognised. Despite herself, in the way dogs do, her tail began to wag slowly, hesitantly.

The soldier seemed to regain more consciousness. His fingers reached under her chest, tickling into her flesh and not quite pinching it. The action had a curious familiarity about it.

'Jet?' he murmured. 'Jet?'

Despite another explosion, which half uprooted the bush beside which she had lain, she heard him. And now she recognised him. She whined, a tiny little whine such as a dog makes when someone teases it with a biscuit. Her tail wagged faster. She licked his hand then his face, her tongue almost frantic with canine joy. She knew the smell now. She knew who this soldier was.

She gripped his battledress with her teeth then, straining her back and pushing hard with her paws, she dragged him fully into the ditch. He groaned loudly as his legs slipped down over some stones: then he passed out.

From the direction of the valley floor there rose into the sky a huge, ominous cloud of black smoke, which billowed wider and wider and rose higher and higher. It blotted out the view of the entire hamlet. A series of dull booms echoed through the hills and the German guns stopped firing. Jet caught a glimpse through the branches of the lemon trees of an aircraft banking and climbing, a white star in a blue circle upon its fuselage.

Small arms fire still issued from the monastery but it was much reduced. The soldiers up the hill had reached the side of the track. In the monastery wall was a wide jagged hole.

Jet ran as fast as she could in the direction of Hogan's position. When she reached it, the pile of stones lay scattered over an area of some square metres. The corporal's body had vanished. Leaning against a nearby tree, from which most of the branches and all of the leaves had been stripped as if, in the middle of summer, this one tree had experienced a private, solitary autumn, was Hogan. His face was ashen. He held his left hand in his right, blood weeping through his fingers.

After a quick lick of Hogan's face to assure him she was all right, Jet took stock of the situation. The firing up the hill had ceased. German soldiers wearing grey uniforms were stumbling through the hole in the wall, their hands above their heads. A stretcher party was stepping off the track towards the lemon trees. Jet set off in their direction, her head held high and her tail straight out behind her.

The sun shone on the khaki canvas of the field hospital tent, mottled by shadows from the trees above. Eight military cots ranged along the side. Orderlies busied themselves with bandages, splints and mugs of hot tea.

Hogan sat on the edge of one of the cots, his hand wrapped in a field dressing and strapped to his chest with a sling made from a length of webbing belt. On the next cot, the soldier from the shallow ditch lay on his back, his cheeks wan. His head was swathed in a pristine white bandage, whilst his entire left leg was encased in field dressings with a tourniquet wound around his thigh. His trousers had been cut from him.

An orderly approached Hogan and handed him a mug of tea, nodding at the adjacent cot.

'Do us a favour, chum,' he said, not realising Hogan was a sergeant. 'Give this mucker here a few sips. We're worked off our feet. Big offensive up north . . .'

Hogan took the mug and, freeing his injured hand, eased the wounded soldier's head up, pressing it to his lips. He took several sips, the tea dribbling down his chin and lay back.

'Thanks, mate,' he said weakly. 'I needed that.'

A scrabbling sound came from the tent wall between the two cots. Hogan glanced down to see Jet's head appear from under the canvas. She had already twice been chased away from the entrance to the tent by the orderlies. Putting the mug down, Hogan leaned painfully over and held up the canvas. Jet crawled through, stood up, shook the dirt off her fur and then, looking at Hogan, snuffled her nose on the other man's hand where it lay by the edge of his cot.

'My dog's taken quite a shine to you,' Hogan remarked as he sipped the tea.

'Your dog?' the wounded soldier queried quietly.

'My dog. Her name's Jess. She's a casualty dog.'

'She's my dog,' the other replied. 'Her name's Jet. She was mine before the war. I trained her. She was,' he moved his head a little from side to side as if ensuring no one else could hear his secret, 'my poaching dog.'

Hogan stared at him.

'I was nabbed,' he went on. 'My dog was requisitioned. I always wondered what happened to her.' He painfully lifted his hand off the cot and held it out to Hogan. 'My name's Parry. Fred Parry.'

Hogan took his hand and said, 'Well, I'll be damned!'

For an hour, Hogan recounted everything that had happened to Jet since he had been her handler and told what he knew of her evacuation from Dunkirk. Fred struggled to keep conscious. The pain in his leg was severe and increased as the dose of morphine he had been given wore off. Finally, he could stand it no longer and the orderly returned, giving him another injection.

Before he drifted into a drugged sleep, he said, 'I reckon the war's over for me now.'

'Me, too,' Hogan replied. 'I've lost a finger.'

'I'll not keep my leg,' Fred remarked matter-of-factly. 'It's smashed to blazes.'

A single tear rolled from the corner of his eye. He hung his hand over the edge of the cot: Jet pushed her head up into it.

'No more wandering the night fields after Sir Arthur's pheasants,' he continued. 'Not a lot a one-legged man can do, is there?'

'There's plenty,' Hogan said. 'After the war there'll be lots of work about.'

'Like what? For a cripple?'

Hogan thought for a minute. He would be all right, would have no difficulty returning to his electrician's business: so he might have to get used to holding a screwdriver a different way but that was all.

'You could do anything,' he said encouragingly. 'Learn a trade. Work in an office. When the war's over, we'll need a lot of men to rebuild the country. Everything from bricklayers and plumbers to doctors and teachers.'

The morphine began to take effect. Fred's eyes grew heavy and he had to fight to remain conscious for just a few more moments.

'And Jet?' he wondered, his eyelids closing. 'Will the war be over for her, too?'

'I'll see to it she's discharged,' Hogan said.

'You promise?' Fred murmured.

Hogan nodded and, even though it meant he would lose his Jess, said, 'Yes, I promise. And I'll see to it you get her back again.'

FINALE

SEPTEMBER 16 1948

For once, the classroom was quiet. Morning sunlight shafted through the windows, lending the colours of the paintings displayed on the wall a harsh clarity. The varnished cloth map of the world hanging next to the blackboard shone like a piece of highly polished furniture.

Form 2 sat in a circle on the floor in front of the teacher's desk. The teacher, a man in his early thirties, sat awkwardly on the edge of the desk, one leg on the floor and the other dangling in the air.

'What happened to Sergeant Hogan?' asked a little girl.

'He went back to his family,' the teacher replied. 'When he was well again, he returned to work with his brother as an electrician. He keeps in touch with Fred and Jet, though. Every summer, on the anniversary of that day outside the monastery of San Martino, he sends Jet a present.'

'What sort of present?' a little boy wanted to know.

'A present a dog would like.'

'What is it?'

'It's a roast chicken,' the teacher answered.

'All to herself?' the little boy stammered, his eyes wide with amazement.

'Yes,' said the teacher. 'All to herself. Except, of course, the bones.'

The children exchanged astonished glances. It seemed incredible to them that a dog should be given a whole roast chicken all to itself. Outside in the playground, a bell rang. The teacher stood up stiffly.

'Right!' he announced. 'Play-time. Line up at the door.'

The children formed two rows, boys on the left and girls on the right. He opened the door and they marched out breaking into a run at the end of the corridor. Yet one child remained behind, a little girl with tousled blonde hair, bright blue eyes and fair skin.

'Sir?' she said tentatively.

'Yes, Ingrid?' the teacher responded.

'Sir, is that story a true story, sir?'

The teacher smiled and answered, 'It might be. What do you think?'

'I don't know,' she replied. Then, seeming to pluck up her courage, she went on, 'Sir, how did you get your metal leg, sir?'

Again, the teacher smiled.

'That's another tale,' he said. 'You run along outside now. Go and get your bottle of milk. You don't want to grow up all weak now, do you?'

'No, sir,' Ingrid agreed, yet she still did not leave the room. Instead, she glanced at the teacher's desk.

'Can I, sir?'

The teacher purported to be mildly exasperated then pretended to give in and said, 'Very well.'

Ingrid walked softly around to the rear of the desk, kneeling down by the chair. In the footwell lay curled a black Labrador cross bitch. She was not a young dog, her muzzle beginning to grey. She was asleep, her paws twitching.

'Why are her feet doing that?' Ingrid whispered.

'She's dreaming,' explained the teacher.

'What about?'

The teacher looked up at the sunshine cutting through the windows. He had a faraway, almost sad, look in his eyes.

'What about?' he repeated quietly. 'I expect she's dreaming about the war.'

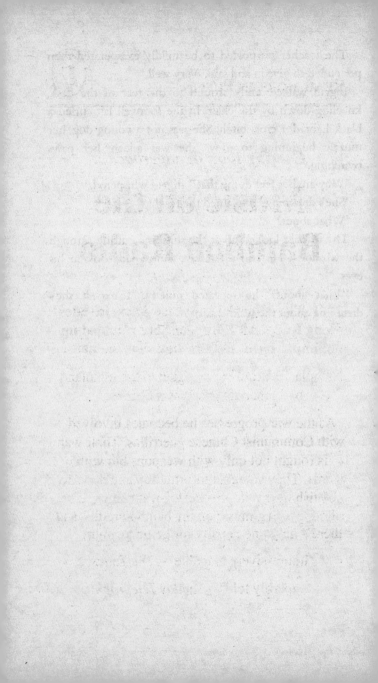

Coming soon in paperback...

Music on the Bamboo Radio

by Martin Booth

1941. The Imperial Japanese Army invades Hong Kong. All Europeans are rounded up and imprisoned. But one boy slips the net ...

Nicholas Holford is smuggled to the mainland of China, disguised as a Chinese.

As the war progresses he becomes involved with Communist Chinese guerrillas. Their war is fought not only with weapons but with words. They smuggle information and news to British troops in prisoner-of-war camps. It's called 'playing music on the bamboo radio' and there's only one penalty for getting caught ...

'impressively readable' – *The Times*

'superbly told' – *Sunday Telegraph*

Johnnie's Blitz

by Bernard Ashley

Wartime London – 'the blitz' – and the East
End was taking a hammering. If it hadn't been
for the gold watch, found hidden in his sock,
Johnnie would have been miles away. But the
watch had got him branded a thief and locked
away with the real criminals.

Still, Johnnie was a survivor. And now he'd
escaped he was going to stay out of trouble.
Until he found himself responsible for someone
small and helpless, who depended on him.
Suddenly it wasn't so easy for Johnnie to look
after Number One.

'An excellent read' – Nicholas Tucker,
Independent

'It's very authentic. It has captured the feel of
the time, I could almost hear the bombs
dropping' – Cyril Demarne OBE, Wartime
Chief Fire Officer, West Ham

Fall-Out

by Gudrun Pausewang

'Your attention, please; this is the police. A nuclear accident took place about ten o'clock this morning inside the Grafenrheinfeld nuclear power station. The population of the entire district is urgently requested to move at once to a closed room and shut all doors and windows. These are precautionary measures. There is no need for anxiety ...'

As the radioactive fall-out gets closer, the government's glib plans for coping with such a disaster collapse. Fourteen-year-old Janna, left alone to look after her little brother in a world gone mad with fear, must make the decisions which will mean life or death for both of them.

'A sobering but totally consuming novel by an excellent writer' – *Sunday Telegraph*

'Hard truths about the effects of fall-out make this book gripping, its message cannot be mistaken' – *School Library Journal*

READ MORE IN PUFFIN

For children of all ages, Puffin represents quality and variety – the very best in publishing today around the world.

For complete information about books available from Puffin – and Penguin – and how to order them, contact us at the appropriate address below. Please note that for copyright reasons the selection of books varies from country to country.

On the worldwide web: www.puffin.co.uk

In the United Kingdom: Please write to *Dept. EP, Penguin Books Ltd, Bath Road, Harmondsworth, West Drayton, Middlesex UB7 0DA*

In the United States: Please write to *Consumer Sales, Penguin USA, P.O. Box 999, Dept. 17109, Bergenfield, New Jersey 07621-0120*. VISA and MasterCard holders call 1-800-253-6476 to order Penguin titles

In Canada: Please write to *Penguin Books Canada Ltd, 10 Alcorn Avenue, Suite 300, Toronto, Ontario M4V 3B2*

In Australia: Please write to *Penguin Books Australia Ltd, P.O. Box 257, Ringwood, Victoria 3134*

In New Zealand: Please write to *Penguin Books (NZ) Ltd, Private Bag 102902, North Shore Mail Centre, Auckland 10*

In India: Please write to *Penguin Books India Pvt Ltd, 706 Eros Apartments, 56 Nehru Place, New Delhi 110 019*

In the Netherlands: Please write to *Penguin Books Netherlands bv, Postbus 3507, NL-1001 AH Amsterdam*

In Germany: Please write to *Penguin Books Deutschland GmbH, Metzlerstrasse 26, 60594 Frankfurt am Main*

In Spain: Please write to *Penguin Books S. A., Bravo Murillo 19, 1° B, 28015 Madrid*

In Italy: Please write to *Penguin Italia s.r.l., Via Felice Casati 20, I–20124 Milano*

In France: Please write to *Penguin France S. A., 17 rue Lejeune, F–31000 Toulouse*

In Japan: Please write to *Penguin Books Japan, Ishikiribashi Building, 2–5–4, Suido, Bunkyo-ku, Tokyo 112*

In South Africa: Please write to *Longman Penguin Southern Africa (Pty) Ltd, Private Bag X08, Bertsham 2013*